MW00377764

THADDEUS STEVENS

Other books by Terry Webb

Manning the Light
Weathering the Storms
Mystery and Mishap
Leaving the Lighthouse
Costly Freedom
Tree of Life

To: Doris M.

T. S. —
Someone
to be proud
of

THADDEUS STEVENS

The Making of an Inconvenient Hero

By Terry Webb

Terry Webb

Copyright 2014 – Terry Webb

All rights reserved.
This book is protected by the copyright laws of the United States of America.
This book may not be copied or reprinted for commercial gain or profit.
The use of short quotations for personal or group study is permitted and
encouraged. Permission will be granted upon request

Historical Fiction

4US

Drawbaugh Publishing Group

444 Allen Drive

Chambersburg, PA 17202

ISBN paperback 978-1-941746-11-0

ISBN eBook 978-1-941746-12-7

For worldwide Distribution, Printed in the U.S.A.

1 2 3 4 5 6 7 8 9 10 11 / 17 16 15 14

Dedication

This story is dedicated to all youth who are bullied because of a disability, are abused, or neglected. *You can be a hero too.*

Table of Contents

Foreword

Thaddeus Stevens was a man well ahead of his time. His commitment to fulfilling the Constitutional promise of liberty resulted in the creation of the sweeping guarantees embedded in the Fourteenth Amendment, the amendment that continues to guide American justice even today.

Like Shakespeare, Stevens kept no diary to record his thoughts or his internal struggles; we have only his work. It is this work that illuminates a compassionate mind combined with incisive political thought.

We applaud Dr. Webb in her efforts to recreate Thaddeus Stevens' youth, here in Vermont, as a way to piece together historical events and his personal life. His impoverished early years, his deformed foot, and his fatherless youth all contributed to his desire to ensure equal opportunity and justice for all citizens. He was a man who chose hope over despair, victory over victimhood, and power over helplessness. In doing so he leaves an inspirational legacy.

For any young student who feels unheard; for any student who is described as disabled; for any student whose parentage is different; for any student whose economic status feels disadvantaged, he or she need only look at Thaddeus Stevens. No one and no social construct defined Thaddeus Stevens. He chose to define himself and to use his intellect to define not only his life but also to improve the lives of his fellow beings.

We are proud of Thaddeus Stevens and thank Dr. Webb for creating and adding to the literature of his life.

Julie Hansen,
Director,
Thaddeus Stevens School, Lyndon Center, Vermont

Acknowledgements

I am grateful to have had the opportunity to spend a week of writing at the Boyd's Mills Highlights Barn and retreat center during the summer of 2013 and to Kent Brown for carrying my boxes and bags into my cabin. I appreciate the patience and guidance of fellow writers and instructors who read and reread my many versions of this book; also thanks to Mary Shafer for her Beta Read and for convincing me to change my voice from first person to third person.

Don Gallagher provided invaluable insight and suggestions as to how to make the manuscript more historically accurate. He also spent evenings proof reading the text from his background as a former middle school English teacher. Julie Hanson, whose vast knowledge of Thaddeus Stevens' life as former teacher and now director of Thaddeus Stevens School, encouraged me to expand on Thad's inner life, his struggles growing up in poverty, and his ambivalent feelings about his alcoholic father. Thank you also to Darlene Colon, who performs the role of Lydia Hamilton Smith and who tweaked a few places in the manuscript.

I am indebted to Paul Choinard, whose story *Thaddeus Stevens in the Limelight* appeared online about the time the movie *Lincoln* became popular. Kathy Brabson first had the courage to write a historical fictional account of Thaddeus Stevens' whole life's accomplishments in her book, *Life of Thad Stevens*. I also appreciate the input of Alex Munro of the Thaddeus Stevens Foundation and Ross Hetrick of the Thaddeus Stevens Society who kept me as historically accurate as possible.

The archivists at the Vermont State Archives and Records Administration, Mariessa Dobrick and Scott Reilly, provided access to the recorded account of the General Assembly session that met in Danville, Vermont in 1805 that is witnessed through the eyes of Thaddeus Stevens as page during that legislative session. The drawing was provided by Paul Carnahan, librarian for the Vermont Historical Society.

I commend Luke McCarthy, a student at the Thaddeus Stevens' school, who spent many hours researching both the topography and clothing to make sure that his drawing of young Thad on horseback surveying the landscape from his farm was as accurate as possible.

Lastly, I want to thank Dean Drawbaugh who never gave up when the process of publishing this work took many different twists and turns.

Introduction

Thaddeus Stevens, ornery and ordinary as an adolescent, grew up to be an influential political leader who made an extraordinary contribution to end slavery in the nineteenth century. Schools and a bridge are now named after him. He convinced others of his belief that creating opportunity for education is the best way to act with compassion. His own experiences growing up taught him that every child, especially those with few advantages in life, should have an equal chance to learn, and then be able to advance themselves. I imagined this story. Many of the events you'll read did not actually occur in real life, but they help us imagine a teen's troubled adolescence and what life was like with his extended family in Danville, Vermont. I created young Thaddeus Stevens' character, mishaps, and adventures when he was thirteen, based on what I knew about him as an adult and from the short paragraphs his biographers wrote about his youth in Vermont.

Today Thaddeus Stevens has become an American hero, thanks to his role in the movie, *Lincoln*, passing the thirteenth amendment to the Constitution, and his many attempts to persuade President Abraham Lincoln to proclaim slaves emancipated during the Civil War.

Now students write essays about his life, create Social Studies exhibits about him, and wonder what his life was like back then when he was close to their age. He never won a popularity contest when he lived. His biographers portrayed him as sharp of tongue and irascible as an adult. In fact, Henry Ward Beecher said of him in a sermon in a Plymouth church in Brooklyn:

"When Thaddeus Stevens shall die his virtues will be better appreciated and his name will be more highly honored than now; for he is one of those men who are very inconvenient when alive and very valuable when dead. It will be remembered that in the dark hours of his country's history when other men were afraid to speak, he was not afraid to speak, and when other men were afraid to be unpopular he was not afraid to be unpopular and did not count his life dear."[1]

As an author I wanted to know how he felt when the other kids bullied him about his disability, his short misshapen club foot. What troubles did he get into that might be like teenagers today? I wanted to know how he became interested in politics and the abolition of slavery.

I chose to write about his early life as a historical fiction story, not narrative fiction, because more than eighty percent of the story is fictional and twenty percent historical, based on known information about early nineteenth century American life in the New England states and what we know about Thaddeus Stevens at this age.

Thaddeus' parents, Sarah Morrill and Joshua Stevens, were married when they both lived in Massachusetts and the couple moved with her Morrill parents and her extended family to settle in the new territory of Vermont. Joshua Stevens was a surveyor, farmer, and cobbler by trade, known for his alcoholic drinking escapades. In 1804 Joshua deserted his family and left his wife, Sarah, saddled with his debts. Her only recourse, as an abandoned wife in nineteenth century America, was to sell their farm and move in with a wealthy cousin, James. If she sold her farm and property she could earn some money to pay off her husband's debts and their boys' education. Living in her cousin's big house and being their housekeeper as well as community nurse became her way to save face. Sarah was a devout Baptist but most of her relatives and other Vermonters were Congregationalists in their religious beliefs.

The Morrills were a close knit family and proud of their revolutionary ancestors. One of Sarah's cousins, Abraham, was the town clerk and as such was connected to local and national politics. In 1805, the year the Vermont legislature met in Danville, Abraham was elected to become Justice of the Peace. Thaddeus' Uncle Abel (James' father) owned the tavern where some of the legislative sessions were held.

Thaddeus Stevens' family exemplified many families in the nineteenth century who suffered due to one member's addiction to alcohol. Even today at least one out of every four children in school classrooms experiences similar trauma. Some live with an addicted parent, a single parent struggling to make ends meet, or an abusive parent. In 1805 Americans believed that drunkenness was a sin. Adult males met at the local tavern, like the local bar today, to drink and gamble. Children in these families take on roles to keep the family stable and one of these roles is the scapegoat child, usually the second child in the family, like Thaddeus, who may become attracted to alcohol or another drug as an adolescent and get into trouble. Thaddeus Stevens' biographers have written the adult Thaddeus liked to gamble and threw away his liquor bottles to control his own drinking. Besides drunkenness, bull-baiting and other forms of gambling were prevalent throughout the nineteenth century.

Thaddeus' interest in the abolition of slavery and slave rights probably was embedded in the Vermont DNA since that state became a slavery free territory in the year 1777. A petition for ending the slave trade occupied center stage during the General Assembly session that met in Danville in 1805.

Two Fugitive Slave Laws were passed by Congress, one in 1793 and one in 1850. The first law required authorities of all states and territories to arrest and return fugitive slaves to their southern masters, fining anyone helping runaway slaves up to five hundred dollars if a station master, as the person helping them was called, was caught. The first law was unpopular in the northern free states. Several states, including Vermont and New York, passed Personal Liberty Laws giving freed slaves the important right of trial by jury.

Early in the nineteenth century northerners helped runaway slaves secretly by harboring them in safe houses. Prior to the Civil War a pattern of escape routes with conductors and safe houses became known as The Underground Railroad. One of the escape routes ran through the northeast part of Vermont. Even though these routes were not established until after 1850, bounty hunters or slave catchers roamed the northeastern states looking for escaping slaves seeking to claim rewards promised by their owners.

Though only a few freed slaves settled in Vermont, researchers Gretchen and Anthony Gerzina uncovered that Abijah Prince and his wife Lucy, freed slaves, settled in Vermont and bought property for a farm. Lucy Prince successfully argued before the Vermont Supreme Court to keep their property under Vermont's Personal Liberty Law. One granddaughter was named Lucy, after her grandmother. She would have been about the same age as Thaddeus. In this story, Thaddeus meets Lucy, the granddaughter, and Lucy's brother, Festus, when they attend the Harvest Festival in Danville. Lucy's father had married a white woman and they settled in Vergennes, not far from Danville. Their children would be mulattos, looked down upon by the rest of society because of racial prejudice. Historians record that many of Thaddeus' female friends in later life were mulattos.

Thaddeus—or Thad as Kathy Brabson in her book, *Life of Thad Stevens*, chose to nickname him— most likely would have attended the legislative sessions in Danville or knew all about them since some of the action took place at his Uncle's tavern. That event could have sparked Thad's life long interest in local and national politics, particularly if his cousin might have chosen him to be a page at the 1805 General Assembly session. However, there is no evidence that he actually was a page.

My goal, as an author, is to inspire pre-teens and teenagers who don't quite fit in with popular kids. I want to encourage them to overcome any disabilities and fears. Having the courage to say what they believe is right could— as studying the life of Thaddeus Stevens demonstrates— change the world around them for the better.

CHAPTER ONE

The Way Life Was

Thad had watched as orange and reds appeared and disappeared behind Lookout Mountain. Nearby leaves whispered to each other on the way to the ground, the only sound disturbing the quiet. This evening Thad rode alone on his horse, Dawn, to get away from what was happening with Pappy. A lump in his throat formed as he thought about Pappy and their family life on the farm.

Before now Pappy and I rode out together to watch the sunset. He'd tell me stories about meeting Mama at a corn husking in Methuen, Massachusetts and other stories of their early days living in Vermont. Not anymore.

Pappy had picked this spot when he surveyed the town of Danville. "This is the best place in all of Vermont for a farm," he told Thad and his older brother, Joshua. "Best house in town," Mama bragged about their farmhouse. Thad and his brothers now filled up the house. Joshua, now fifteen, came first; then Thad, thirteen. After the house was built, Abner, eleven, then Alanson, nine, were born.

Thad's father wanted Thad and Joshua to go with him to the tavern. Mama objected but Pappy said it was their initiation rite as men. They argued and Pappy won. Entering the tavern was like entering a secret cave that's musty and noisy – men spitting tobacco on the floor, drinking, and arguing with each other. Joshua didn't like the atmosphere so he stayed home the next time Pappy wanted his boys to go with him. But Thad continued to tag along.

Usually Thad got bored waiting at the tavern for Pappy to be ready to go home. One day Thad heard cheering coming from behind the tavern. With his curiosity beckoning he went to find out what the cheering was all about. When he opened the back door, he saw a dozen boys gathered around some dogs who were snarling and lunging at a bull tethered to a post. Thad stared at the bull, whose eyes were red and wide and whose nostrils flared and steamed, as he pawed the ground with his hooves. Each time a dog lunged or the bull charged, a boy cheered and threw down a coin. Dirt mixed with blood flew everywhere.

"Hey you. Got ya a dog? Want in?" one boy asked Thad.

Another hooted, "He's just a cripple –probably don't have no money no how."

Thad clenched his fists and his back stiffened. He didn't have any coins but he knew where he could get some. Pappy had coins in his pocket when they arrived. If he still had any after paying for his drinks they'd be in there. Thad hobbled back into the tavern, but he was too late. Mama had Pappy by one arm and was already dragging him toward the door. Pappy dropped the mug of beer he was holding. The beer sprayed on Thad, on Mama, and the floor. Thad helped Mama clean up the mess. Then she shoved Pappy into the back of their wagon and climbed up with Thad. She crossed her arms and her face froze into a scowl. Meanwhile she grabbed the reins and shouted, "Giddyap" to Gerty, their slow draft horse. Thad held on to the sides of the wagon as it lurched toward home.

When they arrived back at the farm, Thad tried to help Mama get Pappy out of the wagon but his father flayed his arms and hit her. All kinds of cuss words spewed from Pappy's mouth. Thad grabbed him around the waist from behind —the nauseating smell of liquor almost choked him — but he managed to pin his father's arms to his sides so he couldn't hurt Mama anymore.

Now this day after breakfast, Pappy harnessed Gerty, hitched her to the wagon, and announced, "I'm going to buy us some sheep." But he hadn't yet come back home with the sheep.

Dusk was now turning the color of the mountain from light green to dark gray. Thad felt gray inside too. He shivered in the cool night air and with his stomach growling he turned Dawn around and headed back to the farmhouse. He nudged Dawn with his thighs, flipped the reins, and rode back to the barn and waiting food. Tall trees on either side of the meadow lined a pathway down from the mountain through the pasture. Rocks sticking out here and there made it hard to plow around. Thad guided Dawn carefully around them so she wouldn't trip. But what Thad heard when he drew close to the barn made his stomach flip-flop.

"Sinner!" Mama's shout ricocheted off the barn wall. "The Bible says not to get drunk and you…you… I've had enough. Get out!"

With his heart racing Thad climbed down off Dawn and rounded the corner of the barn where Joshua sat with his back to the weather-beaten barn wall, his arms around each of their younger brothers. Thad threw Dawn's reins to them and headed for the door of the house just as Pappy stumbled out murmuring, "Aw, Sarah. Can't a man jus' have a few with the men folk?"

Mama went over to Abner and Alanson who were leaning against Joshua's shoulders sobbing, their faces turned away from the door.

"It's going to be all right boys," Mama said in her soothing voice. "Come inside and get your supper." She took Abner and Alanson each by the hand and walked them toward the house.

Thad and Joshua caught Pappy before he fell, guided him into the barn, and plopped him down onto the hay. He smelled like a brewery. Thad's hunger pangs gurgled up in his throat and he felt like puking. Instead, he turned his back on Pappy, sighed, and with Joshua hobbled toward the house and their waiting supper.

The next morning when Thad went to check on him, Pappy was not in the barn and nowhere else around.

CHAPTER TWO

Devil's Mark

Pappy didn't return that day, or the next, or the next.

"Bet he's at the tavern," Thad said to Mama the night after the bill collectors started coming.

"Well, you are not going there," she spit out. "Don't need him back here creating more debt. Looks like we're going to have to sell this farm to pay back what he owed."

"No!" Thad and his brothers chorused.

"You and Pappy love this land," Thad managed through clenched teeth, resistance crawling up his spine. *Never to see the sunsets over Lookout Mountain. Never to go hunting in the woods,* he grieved. *No!* He wished to shout out again and again.

Joshua added, "I can make shoes and boots. Pappy taught us how."

But Mama announced that she had already made plans for them to move in with Cousin James and his wife Cathy in town.

"Why them?" Thad practically screamed out his question.

"Why not our grandparents or Cousin Abraham?"

Mama put her hands on her hips and looked right into Thad's eyes and replied, "Because they have the biggest house."

Since Cousin James owned the grist mill that straddled over Joe Brook and many other businesses, he did have a larger house than their other relatives, Thad reasoned. Almost all the houses in town were owned by one or another of their Morrill relatives. But Cousin James was the richest of all his relatives; his family, the poorest. Thad hated being poor and having to sell their farm.

The next day when Thad woke up, he found Mama had already gathered up some of their household items that they might need. All Thad's arguments and his brothers' had been in vain. Mama told them to pack up their clothes and any treasures they wanted to bring. By noon they had managed to load their belongings onto their farm wagon. With their cow, Nellie, tied behind the wagon, they left their farm and headed into town. Thad rode Dawn with Alanson sitting behind holding onto him.

Cousin Cathy opened the door and gave Mama a hug. She then led the five of them upstairs to where they would be sleeping.

"You four boys can have this room at the top of the stairs," she told them, "but two of you will have to share a bed. Your mother will sleep with Susan and Catherine at the other end of the hall."

Thad thought that Cousin James' house didn't seem so big anymore with all five Stevens adding to the four Morrill cousins occupying every space.

He slept fitfully the first night in his new bed. He missed their farm. And he couldn't seem to escape from the cobwebs in his dream. They tightened around him like chains locking his feet into place when he tried to hurry. Darkness still hovered over the bed he shared with Joshua when he heard the ringing.

Dang that bell. Must be four o'clock and time to get up. I just need to finish my dream. Thad buried his head under the covers to drown out Mama's wake-up bell and its dong dong loud ringing.

Joshua yanked off the coverlet. Now that his misshapen foot was exposed, Thad sat up cursing under his breath so Mama couldn't hear him. He knew she'd box his ears if she heard him saying any cuss words. *But Pappy's cuss words are a lot worse than mine.*

"Wake up brother." Joshua punched Thad in the ribs.

"Ouch!" Thad punched him back and they went at it.

The bell rang again, this time louder closer. Mama loved to ring that big cow bell. Thad wanted to grab it and throw it in the nearby brook.

"Stop fighting boys. Get up and get dressed."

Mama's face and features stood out like a ghost's in the candle light with the sound of her voice muffled. Out of one eye Thad saw her place the lit candle on the nightstand between their beds. Joshua's suspenders snapped as he pulled on his pants.

"Give me another minute," Thad mumbled into his pillow, "Just let me finish my dream."

"No. Time's a-wasting," Mama's voice said again.

Thad heard her call to Abner and Alanson in the bed next to theirs. They were still snoozing away. Thad wondered what they were dreaming.

"Hurry! Got to get to your chores."

Thad reached under his side of the bed and groped for his boots, knowing he'd come out at the little end of the horn if he didn't obey. He hated putting on his boots. His feet had gotten too big and his toes cramped something fierce when he wore them. Walking in them made it even more painful because of his club foot.

My strange foot. Abner and Alanson have normal feet. But not Joshua and me. Why only us? We're older than Abner and Alanson. Mama has told us that she depends on Joshua and me since Pappy left. How can we be dependable with these feet? My left leg is shorter than my right and it doesn't have any heel – it sort of hangs from my ankle. Both Joshua's feet are crooked – his toes are pointed inward. When we walk, we can't help our limp. But Thad didn't want to think about that. He felt like disappearing when he heard the jibes and barbs behind his back.

"Devil's left his mark," the other kids taunted. *As if we'd done something bad enough to displease God to deserve these club feet.* Thad asked himself that question every morning. Mama sighed when either he or Joshua asked her, then mumbled, "God knows," or "Got to learn to live with that thorn in your flesh like the Apostle Paul." Pappy said, "Being born with those feet t'weren't your fault. I'm the one to blame."

It seemed to Thad that Pappy blamed Mama as much as she blamed him. She usually gave his pappy a disgusted look when he came home after drinking. Then he told her to stop nagging and they would argue. *Maybe their fighting all the time caused our feet to be like they are,* Thad often thought.

But his father disgusted Thad too— especially when he was drunk. At those times Thad wished this man weren't his father. At other times...

well that was different. He missed their times of riding together to watch the sunset, of playing chess in the evenings, and wrestling. But when Pappy had been drinking, Thad wished he would just go away. Thad thought Pappy read his mind since he thought that so much recently and that's why he left this time. He probably didn't like Mama nagging him either. Thad wanted the old Pappy back. *If I didn't have this club foot, if I behaved better... maybe that would make him stop drinking.* Thad wished he'd had the nerve to tell him that before he left.

"Wash up and get to your milking," Mama said to him. Thad's chore every morning was to milk Nellie.

They only had one pitcher and one basin so Thad and his brothers had to take turns washing. Abner got there first. He had two good feet. His and Alanson's chores were to bring in the wood from the shed for keeping the fires going in the two fireplaces on the chimney that straddled the kitchen and the parlor. Joshua's chore was to go to the well for water. Fortunately the well was close by since Joshua had a harder time walking than Thad.

Thad went to the barn to milk Nellie. But he knew that if he had to carry the full pail back to the house it would spill since he couldn't walk straight. Sure enough, Cousin James thought so too.

"Clumsy oaf!" Cousin James shouted when Thad came through the door with the pail spilling milk all over the sandy floor. Thad decided that in the future he'd talk Abner into carrying the full pail.

Pappy had made special boots to wear on their club feet, and canes for both Joshua and Thad to help them balance and keep from falling. Joshua managed with two canes and even then waddled along like a duck. Thad dragged one foot behind him. He wished he could run like Abner and Alanson but whenever he tried he tripped and fell so he quit trying. That's why Mama had insisted to Pappy that he have his own horse.

Mama said she had to sell all the animals when she sold the farm. Thad pleaded with her to keep his Dawn.

"She'll probably bring the most money," she replied, "Besides, now that we're staying at Cousin James' house which is close to the town center you can walk everywhere."

Thad tried walking into town with Joshua to go to Mrs. Hicks' school.

But they both got so tired and the other kids pointed fingers at the way they walked. When they heard laughter behind them, Thad turned around and saw several boys and girls imitating his limp and Joshua's waddling. His stomach tied up in knots. His fists went up ready to fight.

"Don't!" Joshua gripped his arm. "You know they'll gang up on us. Try and ignore them."

So the next day Joshua asked Cousin James to take the two of them in his buggy. Thad convinced him by saying the route they walked was on his way to the mill and wasn't he going that way anyway? Thad then pushed Abner to stand in front of him and sweetened the deal by saying that Abner could help Cousin James on the weekends at the mill. Abner stuck out his tongue at Thad.

"I'm not taking the young'uns," Cousin James responded. "They can walk a straight line."

"But Abner can run the mill wheel. He's strong."

After Cousin James finally agreed he made Thad hitch up his buggy. Now that he had boys to help with men's chores he could find all kinds of reasons to have Thad and his brothers do everything he used to do—except running the mill.

CHAPTER THREE

Parlor School

Well into his second week staying at Cousin James', Thad had mastered the rhythm of milking Nellie. He watched the milk splash into the pail as a way to take his mind off his pinching feet that were squeezed into his too small boots. As he milked he sang a song Grandpappy's people had sung to him when he was a little boy.

"In freedom we're born, and in freedom we'll live!
Our purses are ready,
Steady, friends, steady;
Not as slaves, but as free men, our money we'll give."

Abner, who had by now forgiven Thad for making him work at the mill, joined in. The cow swished her tail to the sound of the music. When the milk pail was full, Abner carried it into the house. Droplets of rain were beginning to fall from black clouds as they both reached the door and closed it when it started to pour. Abner handed the pail of milk to Cousin Cathy and he and Thad joined the others at the breakfast table. They slid onto the bench beside their brothers.

Thad thought, *First thing, I need to get these boots off. Ah...h. Now I can wiggle my toes.*

Mama grimaced at him from the other side of the table where she sat with the Morrill twin girls.

Thad didn't know much about girls when they moved in. Mama used to say she wished one of her sons would have been a girl but instead was blessed with boys. Now she braided the girls' hair every morning and grinned when one of them giggled. Thad scowled thinking about Mama. She didn't smile much now when she was with him and his brothers. Instead, she made them memorize verses from the Bible.

"Why doesn't Cousin Cathy make her girls memorize bible verses?" Thad asked her.

"Not as important for girls to be educated as boys. Besides, they're Congregationalists and we're Baptists. Baptists need to memorize the Bible."

Thad tried ignoring the twins most of the time but that became impossible since he was with them every day for meals and school. Anyway, since they were only six, they were closer to Alanson's age then his.

He spooned down his porridge and grabbed a sausage before anyone else, pushed his chair away from the table, grabbed his cane for balance and stood up. He needed to get to the parlor first so he could get the seat closest to the fireplace on that side of the chimney to warm up his cold feet.

"May I...." Thad didn't even get the whole "be excused please" out of his mouth before Mama replied, "Please, take your dishes over to the sink, Thad, and I'll meet you in the parlor." She nodded her head when she gave him the excusing order.

They didn't have parlor school every day since all able bodied boys were needed to help with the harvesting, except on rainy days. This week, because of all the rain, they had more schooling than farming.

Mama had announced at breakfast that Thad and his brothers would learn inside today instead of gathering hay for racks outside. The fields were too muddy. When Thad worked, the men let him ride one of the draft horses meant for pulling the wagon instead of walking the fields. When Joshua asked how they would get to Mrs. Hicks' school, Mama answered, "Mrs. Hicks took sick so we'll have parlor school here."

Thad slowly made his way through the doorway by the chimney toward one of the two chairs closest to the warm fire. There he could sit and wait for his brothers and cousins to take their seats on other chairs and sofas and for Mama to come and be their teacher.

Thad slid his backside into the rear of the stiff chair —or tried to. He squirmed, arched his back, and rested his long limbs on the chair arms. But his hands hung awkwardly over the edge of the chair arms and he had to stick his legs out in front or pull them back under the chair. So he shuffled his feet back and forth. No matter what he did he still couldn't make his lanky frame comfortable. He tried to distract his discomfort by listening to the drops of rain on the window pane while he waited. The rain sounded like beats of a drum when the drops hit the window.

Joshua waddled in and sat down opposite Thad in the other straight backed chair beside the fireplace.

When Mama came into the parlor, Thad complained, "I don't know why Joshua and I have to be with all our younger cousins and their friends in parlor school anyway. Most of what goes on in parlor school is boring. I can already multiply and divide and read anything I can find." Mama ignored him.

Thad leaned over and poked Joshua, hoping he would back him up but Joshua remained silent. Instead, he sat at attention like a good soldier. So Thad went back to trying to sit in the hard chair. He moved to the edge of the chair trying to get his long legs way under it to hide his foot. But his feet were cold away from the fire so he tried scrunching against the back of the chair and sticking his legs out to get them closer to the fire. Up and under, back and out. Mama bustled about. Thad made humming noises to the rhythm of his feet.

"Quiet," Mama called out. "Now open your primers to the Lord's Prayer. We will recite it together."

"Our Father, who art in heaven, hallowed be Thy name. Thy kingdom come…" He recited by rote with the others, his mind elsewhere.

"Thad," Mama turned to him when they were finished reciting. "Will you please read James, chapter two, verses two through six from the Bible?"

Relieved not to have to sit any longer in the uncomfortable chair, Thad stood up, balanced himself with his cane, and reached out to pick up the treasured old leather book from its special spot on the round table by the fireplace. It even smelled ancient. His hands touched the sacred book, tracing the gold lettering with his fingers on its cover. His hands were rough but the leather covering on the book was smooth. He ruffled through its centuries old pages of stories, not sure where to find the story that James wrote. Was it in the beginning in the Old Testament or the New? He raised his eyes to meet Mama's. She answered his question even though he hadn't asked it out loud.

"You'll find it toward the end of the New Testament, after Hebrews." Embarrassed by the snickers from his younger brothers and cousins, Thad located the passage. After all he was supposed to be the smart one.

He read: "…Hath not God chosen the poor of this world rich in faith and heirs of the kingdom which he hath promised to them that love him?"

After he'd read the last verse, Thad started to close the Bible until he saw the inscription on the front page, Mama and Pappy's names and their wedding date. His name and his brothers as well as their birthdates were on the next page. His heart slowed its beat and he squished his eyes closed to keep from crying. Then he carefully put the big book back in its special place on the table. He turned to Mama, thinking she'd now start saying her usual words about how they were special to God because they were so poor, having to sell not only their farm but Dawn too. *But if God favored the poor over the rich why work to make money in the first place? Pappy never worried about it. He bought whatever he wanted.*

"Education," started another one of Mama's sayings. "That's the golden key that will unlock any door." She said that many times too. The word "key" made Thad remember where Mama hid the key to unlock the padlock on the door at their farmhouse that no one had bought yet. He wished he was there now with only his immediate family. When she spouted those words, Thad was never sure which door she meant, the door out of Cousin James' house, the door into Heaven since they were believers, or the door to being rich.

Mama snapped Thad's attention back into the room by talking about a book he'd never seen before. "Cousin Abraham asked me to give you this book written by Dr. David Ramsey on the American Revolution to read and study. He says it's time you both learned all about why winning the war against the British was important. Many men-folk, some of your Pappy and my kin among them, sacrificed their lives for the principles

of the Revolution. Joshua, since I need you to help me with the younger
children today I'm going to give this book to Thad. He'll have the first
chance to read and study the book since he reads fast. Thad, when you
finish it and prepare a report, you can give the book to Joshua to read and
study."

This was Thad's lucky day! A new book to read! They didn't have
many books to read except the Bible, Pilgrim's Progress, and Paradise
Lost, and he certainly didn't want to study another hornbook or prim-
er. Thad had read those silly rhymes such as "A: After Adam's Fall, We
Sinn'd All" so many times he could chant each one in his sleep.

"Go on," Mama said, "You can take the history book with you to read
anywhere in this house until time for dinner."

Thad took the new book carefully from Mama and clasped it tightly
to his chest as if it could open right into his heart and from there to his
brain. Then he tucked it carefully under his left arm as he stood up, bal-
ancing his club foot with his cane. He glanced over to Joshua.

"A whole morning to read," he gloated.

As he escaped from the parlor, Joshua gave Thad his dagger look,
piercing right through him. When Thad left, he overheard Mama asking
his brothers and the twins to help her pass out the writing slates to the
other children.

*Now I don't have to listen to them recite their ABCs or hear them
scratching the words that Mama calls out to them to write on their slates.*

Cousin Abraham often talked about Dr. Ramsey. He had showed
Thad an article Dr. Ramsey had written titled, "Advantages of the
Revolution," and shared its ideas: about America being a political
experiment, what becoming independent from British rule meant, as well
as the importance of having a free press and being able to say and believe
whatever one wanted to say and believe. Thad could still remember what
that article said, almost word for word:

*"The world will soon see the result of an experiment in politics, and be
able to determine whether the happiness of society is increased by religious
establishments, or diminished by the want of them…In establishing American
Independence the pen and press had merit equal to that of the sword."*[2]

Thad wondered about Dr. Ramsey's questioning whether or not having churches and other places of worship made people happier. Mama made Thad and his brothers attend the Baptist Church every Sunday with her. *Maybe we'd be happier if we didn't attend, like Pappy, or weren't forced to attend like my brothers and me. Pappy doesn't always attend. He goes to the tavern to drink instead. When he is drinking he seems happier but Mama, my brothers and I certainly aren't.*

When Thad looked up from his thoughts, he spied the rocking chair near the hearth and started to sit down with his new book.

"No you don't! That's my knitting chair," Cousin Cathy shouted. "Upstairs with you!"

Looking longingly at the chair that might fit his lengthening backbone, Thad turned around and headed for the stairs to their second floor bedroom. Once there he closed the door and flung himself on the bed he shared with Joshua. With the drumming of the rain on the roof above providing a rhythm, he started reading:

"The English Colonists were, from their first settlement in America, devoted to liberty, on English ideas, and English principles. They not only conceived themselves to inherit the privileges of Englishmen, but though in a colonial situation, actually possessed them..."[3]

We are still English in our ideas and the way we live, even though we call ourselves Americans. When Thad asked Grandpappy Morrill about why they still did things the way the English did, he'd said, " Even though we have English ways of speaking and living, now we don't have to pay the unfair British taxes and we can absorb different ways of living, such as the way Poles or Germans or Spaniards live."

Grandpappy had told Thad about his close friendship with the Polish engineer, Thadeusz Kosciuszko, who lined up the canons for fortification in General Washington's army. President George Washington made Thadeusz a general and granted him American citizenship. Pappy said that General Kosciuszko came to visit Grandpappy on his way out west shortly before Thad was born. That's why his pappy decided to name him Thaddeus. On Thad's eighth birthday, Grandpappy gave him a gold coin with the General's picture on it. Thad kept the coin on his bed stand. Since he had long rust colored bushy hair, he let it grow to look just like the General's. When he was ten years old, Pappy had told Thad that President Jefferson called General Thadeusz the "Purest Son of Liberty." Thad wanted to someday earn that kind of honor too.

CHAPTER FOUR

Boot Making

Thad was still pondering the meaning of what Ramsey said about the American colonists when Mama's cowbell rang again. This time the dong dong came from the bottom of the stairs.

Under British rule the colonists thought of themselves as free and independent even though they weren't free. And they had equality of rank and position – no Kings or Nobles. The English people who came to this new country to live and work really believed that here on this continent all men were by their very nature equal.

With the thoughts of Ramsey's writings lodged in his brain, Thad hid the new book under his pillow, picked up his cane, hobbled toward the stairs, and started down stopping half way down when a new thought made him pause. *What about slaves? They weren't free? But they should be. At least Vermonters thought so since they banned slavery in 1777.*

Cooking smells of pungent cabbage dismissed any more lofty thoughts. Thad's mouth moistened and his stomach grumbled. He looked down over the banister to see Cousin Cathy putting the steaming pot in the middle of the table. Everyone was seated except him— even Joshua. Thad and Joshua were usually last to be seated. Even the twins were seated, their meal preparation under Cousin Cathy's direction completed. Girls' education took place mainly in the kitchen with the other women.

Thad noted that Cousin James was looking up at him from his place at the head of the table, his usual scowl on his face. He had his spoon and knife up and his pewter plate ready to get his food out of the kettle pot.

"If we're now all ready," he said, still glaring as Thad sat down on the end of the bench. Cousin James bowed his head and said grace. After helping himself to a portion of corned beef, cabbage, potatoes, and carrots from the pot of food, he nodded toward Cousin Cathy who spooned some on to the twins' plates and then passed the large spoon to Mama as he announced, "Mr. Ashley stopped by the mill today and told me that he needed some new boots for his boys. So as soon as you open the shop, one of you boys go fetch him." All this he said between bites, while looking directly at where Thad and Joshua were sitting.

Thad stared back at him while he spooned his portion from the food left in the pot. He hadn't even started to eat his food and he was starving! He knew if he were allowed he'd eat all the food in that pot. Even after he finished eating his small portion, his stomach still grumbled and he really wanted more.

He was considering his reply to Cousin James when Joshua spoke first.

"Can't Thad go fetch him while I start the cobbling?"

Thad thought, *He's only trying to get back at me because I got to read the new book first.* He had a sudden urge to clobber his older brother. Instead, he said to Cousin James, "Anything to suit your majesty."

"What insolence!" Cousin James' face contorted and he started to get up out of his chair.

Mama came to Thad's rescue, ignoring his sassy response. "James, I think Alanson can go to Mr. Ashley's in this rain faster than Thad can."

Thad held his breath waiting for Cousin James to come around the table to thrash him. Instead, Cousin James sat back in his chair and continued eating.

Taking that to mean yes to Mama's proposition, Thad finished eating what was on his plate. He reached under the table for his boots that he'd left there. He could hear his stomach talking to him. But he knew better than to ask for more than his allotted share and he had to put the boots on to walk to the carriage house next door adjacent to the barn and the main house. That's where their cobbler tools were kept.

Shoe and boot making and fixing had become one of his family's sources of income— that and Mama's housekeeping. Cousin James even allowed them to hang a sign on the corner of the building that read, *Cobbler Shop.*

Thad needed Joshua's help in finishing his own new boots while they waited for Mr. Ashley to come. He had cut the soles out yesterday. The soles sat on the lasts or wooden molds that helped shape the shoe. The deerskin leather still needed to be burnished.

"May I please be excused?" Thad asked Cousin James who nodded and turned to Alanson. "And you too. Go fetch Mr. Ashley."

"You can come back to the mill with me," he said, turning to Abner.

With his feet squeezed into his old boots—for the final time he hoped— Thad picked up his cane, jacket, and cap and headed out into the rain. Spit. Splat. Splatter. The rain hit the ground and made puddles. Now that he didn't care about the old boots, Thad waded right through the puddles, the pain from his club foot shooting up his leg.

The tawny smell of leather hit his nose when he opened the barn door. Cousin James had given Thad and Joshua permission to hang Pappy's shoemaking equipment against one wall. His carriage house was large for holding many carriages and sleighs he rented and sold. Their small space was only big enough to put their lasts, a bench, a chair and a small table where the boys had placed their knives, pincers, hammer, a glazing iron, awl, and thread below where they had hung the leather skins. Grandpappy had given Mama some money to purchase new leather from the tanner.

Thad really didn't like shoe and boot making the same way Joshua did but he couldn't stand wearing his cramped boots any longer. And where was his slow brother? Finally, Joshua shuffled through the door.

"Do you need help, Thad?"

"Could you burnish the leather hide for me?"

"Will this do?" Joshua took down a dark brown hide from its nail and started rubbing it with his glazing tool. After the leather was smooth and shiny he handed the dark piece to Thad who measured and cut it, made holes with the awl, and prepared to start sewing. He was ready with the needle when he heard footsteps outside.

"Come in," Joshua called.

Two boys about nine and eleven years old stepped inside. Mr. Ashley, his burly body filling up the doorway, pushed the two boys into the room and cleared his throat.

"Ahem. Here're me boys who need new boots for winter. I'll pay you a quarter for each." He put the coins down on the table.

"No trouble," Joshua replied nodding to the boys. "I'll measure your feet, first." He cut some parchment paper, laid two pieces side by side on the floor, and asked each boy to stand on the pieces. Taking a knife from the table he cut out the shape of the boys' feet from the paper, making the patterns he'd need to shape the soles.

While Joshua was down on the floor cutting carefully around the boys' shoes for the right fit, Thad focused on the coins Mr. Ashley had placed on the table right next to the tarred twine he'd been using for sewing up his new boots. Thad's hand reached out to grasp the twine and somehow managed to capture the coins with the twine. He dropped the coins into his pocket and threaded the stiff needle, completed the sewing, then admired his finished product.

Thad tugged to pull off his old boots from his cramped toes while the Ashley boys were putting on their coats. Mr. Ashley shooed each boy out the door.

"Be back tomorrow," he called as Joshua rose and hobbled over to close the door.

Meanwhile, Thad had pulled on a new boot over each foot —even his ugly one— and was standing up. *They fit! Now I'm ready to be on my way.*

"Where are you going?" Joshua asked when he turned around and almost bumped into Thad who, with his new boots on and cane in hand, looked like he was ready to leave.

"Going to look for Pappy at the tavern. I'll be back in an hour when you're ready to sew."

"But we've barely started," Joshua protested. "And Mama told us not to go back there!" But Thad brushed past him and closed the door before his brother could protest any more.

Thad looked up and down the road and pondered how to get to the tavern. Although the rain had now stopped, the road was a sea of mud and puddles. He didn't really want to get his new boots muddy but the tavern was farther down the road. *Maybe I'll find Pappy there if I'm lucky.*

It's worth the risk of a scolding from Mama. And my new boots really need to be broken in to make sure they're waterproof. Then his logical mind made him hesitate. *If I wait a little longer for a buggy or wagon to pass by I could get a ride.*

Seeing no buggies or wagons around, he started walking carefully down the road to the tavern, dipping his cane into each puddle to measure the depth so he could decide whether to walk through it. He skirted the ones that were too deep and crisscrossed the road to avoid those places. He became so occupied trying to find the driest place to cross the road to avoid the puddles that he didn't see or hear the horse and wagon behind him.

"Thad, that you? Want a ride?"

He turned around to see Mama's Cousin Abraham.

"The Sergeant comes to my rescue!" Thad saluted and then climbed up to sit beside his favorite cousin.

"Where're you off to foot soldier in distress?"

Since he'd known him, he and Cousin Abraham had played soldier together, reliving the great battles of the Revolution.

"Off to yonder tavern to rescue Pappy from the evil brew."

Cousin Abraham's usual jovial face fell and he frowned.

"Think he might still be in the battle."

"Or he might be wounded."

They both fell silent, lost in their thoughts while listening to the clip-clop of the draft horse as he splattered his way through the mud and puddles. Cousin Abraham pulled in the reins in front of the tavern.

"I'll drop you off here and go on my way to the courthouse to file some deeds. I'll come back to fetch you and your Pappy, if he's here, when I'm finished."

CHAPTER FIVE

Bull-Baiting

Smoke stung Thad's eyes when he opened the door to the cavernous tavern. Uncle Abel came from behind the bar where a keg surrounded by pewter mugs rested.

"What can I do for you, Thad?"

"Have you seen Pappy?"

"Not since the day your Mama came and dragged him home. Thought he was staying out of trouble."

"He! He! Probably sleeping it off in a hay stack somewhere," one of the men standing nearby remarked.

Thad's shoulders sagged. He sighed. *Where are you Pappy?*

Thad made his way around the spittoons, stepping around mounds of tobacco and cigar stubs until he reached the back door. He tried opening it but something on the other side resisted.

"Hey, watch it!" The door flung open and something turned into an arm with a fist ready to punch.

"Sorry."

Thad moved to one side. The fist unclenched and the arm disappeared.

Thad noted the tethered bull.

"Game still on?" he asked tentatively, wondering whether the bull was the same one as before but thought, *the other's probably dead by now or let loose and a new bull brought in.* Blood oozed from this bull from several wounds. Thad assumed the wounds were from dog bites. But no dogs were present.

"Sure." The voice came from behind the open door. A face on a head of straggly hair peeked around the door frame.

"Got your coins, Gimpy? Game will begin when Zach and Tom get here with the two pups. One of the other dogs got killed. Bull sure got him."

Thad swallowed the insult and kept his eyes on the tethered bull.

"Is that a new bull?"

"Since when?" the head said.

Thad guessed these boys didn't remember him or weren't there when he came with Pappy. If he'd managed to get the coins from Pappy's pocket, he'd have bet on that bull. This bull didn't seem to have much energy. His head drooped and his eyes were glazed. *Poor bull. He looks like a loser. I've come to your rescue,* he imagined whispering to the bull so the boys present couldn't hear him. *When I bet on you, you'll know you can fight so you can beat those dogs.*

"Have a swig." A skinny body attached to another head appeared holding up a pitcher and a pewter mug. "And sit a spell." He beckoned Thad to join him and the other boys seated or squatting waiting for the dogs to arrive.

Remembering that Cousin Abraham said he'd pick him up, Thad hesitated.

"Here. Try it. Won't hurt you. Put hair on your chest," said the boy holding out the mug.

Leaning on his cane, Thad reached for the mug. The bull bellowed. *Maybe he's fiercer than I thought.* Thad swallowed.

Panting and pattering hounds came from around the corner of the tavern. They growled when they saw the bull and strained forward pulling their handlers, the two boys holding their leads. Thad thought they looked familiar.

"Throw down your coins and declare your bets." The boy with the scraggly head of hair declared the start of the game.

"The bull!" Thad shouted. He took one of the coins out of his pocket and tossed it on the ground.

Each of the other boys shouted a name and threw a coin down next to Thad's. He guessed the names belonged to the dogs.

"Go get 'im!" commanded one of the boys as he untied the collar around his hound's neck. The dog bared his teeth and ran toward the bull. It pawed the ground and bellowed louder. The second dog's hair stood up on his back. He arched it, like a snake would coil getting ready to strike.

Thad's belly welcomed the warm liquid. He drank some more, taking more of the foaming liquid from the pitcher as it was passed around. Tasted good. Adrenaline now rushed through his body. He was cheering on the bull. Every muscle was in tune with the bull who was gathering up enough energy to fend off his enemies.

The bull bent his head down and kicked out his hooves as the hounds rushed toward him. A crowd gathered and the noise rose. Boys shouted. Dogs barked. The bull brayed. Everyone yelled and cheered. More liquor appeared and Thad filled his mug again and again. One with the crowd, everything around him became blurry. He dropped his cane and swung his club foot back and forth.

Thad lost his balance and fell backwards. A hand gripped one elbow and a voice said, "Steady, lad. Let's go."

Another voice said, "No harm done. Let him stay."

The cheering and shouting grew louder. Thad couldn't hear what the voices near him were arguing about any longer.

Suddenly the cheering stopped.

"That's my bull!" Another voice shouted. "I'll shoot whoever stole him!"

Bang... then blackness.

Thad woke. His head throbbed. His stomach heaved. Scenes came creeping back in flashes. The bull? Did I win my bet? Am I shot? The backs of his cousin and uncle were all he could see in the dusk. His mouth felt like parchment. He leaned over the side of the wagon and threw up.

The wagon stopped in front of Cousin James' house and Cousin Abraham turned around and asked Thad, "Can you make it into the house on your own?" Thad nodded with effort. His head felt like it would split in two. He found his cane and gingerly climbed down - inching like a snail and using his cane for balance. He looked up and saw Cousin James standing in the doorway, his arms crossed on his chest and his lips pressed together in a thin line. Mama stood beside him, her mouth equally as grim.

Behind Thad his Uncle Abel said, "Best for him to sleep it off."

"Get!" Cousin James commanded and pointed to the stairs. "You're confined to this house." Speaking to the others he said through clenched teeth, "Chip of the old block."

Thad kept his head lowered as he passed them all, hobbled up the stairs and collapsed onto the bed into oblivion.

CHAPTER SIX

Paying the Piper

The bed springs' squeaking disrupted Thad's intoxicated sleep. He opened one eye to see a body in bed beside him. He whispered to it, "Pappy wasn't there." His brother, Joshua, spit out damning words one at a time, "You stink. You… stole… our money."

Thad felt the heavy guilt in the bottom of his heart. He knew he was in a pickle.

Next the dong dong of Mama's cow bell reverberated in his sore head. He covered his ears to muffle the vibrations.

"Time for chores. Tub for you, Thad. Abner and Alanson— dress for racking hay today." Mama had a tub full of warm water ready. Thad slipped his hurting body down into the water to soak the guilt away.

Guess I do stink, like Pappy did when he came home drunk. Don't like smelling myself anymore then I liked smelling Pappy when he drank the stuff. As a matter of fact, I don't like myself much for drinking the stuff. Wish I could have said no. But if I had said, "No," the other boys would have called me names.

Abner had already started milking Nellie when Thad arrived. While Thad milked he followed the drip-dripping into the pail and said soothing words to Nellie, really meant to comfort his own raw nerves.

At the breakfast table, he avoided looking at Mama, Cousin James, or Joshua, fearing they'd accuse him with their eyes.

Cousin James excused Abner, Alanson, and the twins, Susan and Catherine, and then said, "Thad, your Mother and I want to talk to you.

Joshua, I'm asking you to join us in the parlor."

Thad felt awful enough without anticipating an interrogation. His head felt so heavy! He really didn't want any more of Mama's or Cousin James' lectures. *If Pappy were here he'd understand.*

He followed Joshua into the parlor, surprised to find Uncle Abel and Cousin Abraham already seated side by side on the settee. Joshua dropped down first in one of the straight chairs by the fireplace. Thad slid back as far as he could in the other stiff chair, shuffled his feet in and out, folded and unfolded his hands. Mama sat down next to Cousin James.

"Thad," Mama began, "Why did you do it?"

Thad shrugged his shoulders.

"Pappy wasn't there. I was waiting for Cousin Abraham and the kids invited me to join the game."

"But I told you not to go to the tavern!"

Joshua hissed, "You stole the money that Mr. Ashley paid us for making his boys' new boots. You told me you'd be back but left me to make the boots by myself."

Cousin Abraham turned to Mama and said, "Sorry, Sarah. It took me longer than I thought at the courthouse."

Uncle Abel said, "Boys will be boys, Sarah. No harm done, really."

Mama's icy stare chilled Thad. He was still waiting for his sentence— for someone to tell him what his punishment would be.

Cousin James at last gave his verdict.

"Thad, we don't need another drunk in this family. Therefore, there will be no more of these trips to the tavern. You will not be permitted outside this house for a month, except to help Joshua in the cobbler shop. And you will earn twice the value of the money you took so as to atone for your theft."

"And you will memorize ten bible verses a week," Mama added.

Now Thad really felt streaked.

"Tarnation, Mama! You usually whitewashed all Pappy's wrongdoings. You didn't make him memorize bible verses when he got drunk. Why me?"

Cousin Abraham said to Cousin James. "James, could you shorten the house arrest by a few weeks?" Then turning to Mama, he said, "Sarah, there's a reason I was late picking up Thad. It's because when I got to the courthouse, I opened a letter with a reminder that Danville is the town where the Vermont legislature will be meeting two weeks from today. We all have to get ready. Thad would learn a great deal by being a page."

All eyes and ears in the room moved from Thad to Cousin Abraham.

"The delegates will meet in the courthouse and the tavern until their business has been completed. But in addition to the beds on the second floor of the tavern, I'll need all Danville residents to provide lodging for at least two delegates. James, do you think you could keep several of the delegates here? Sarah, could you provide lodging and meals at your farmhouse since it hasn't sold yet? The lodgers will pay you, of course."

Whew, Thad thought. All except for the memorization bit, two weeks more of living in this house would not be such a bad punishment after all.

CHAPTER SEVEN

Making Amends

Even though Cousin James agreed to shorten Thad's sentence, Mama didn't give in on memorization. Thad still had to recite the bible verses at the supper table.

He started with the first verse from Proverbs twenty: "Wine is a mocker and beer a brawler." *What does wine have to do with anything? I was drinking beer,* Thad thought.

During the first week, Thad memorized and recited all the verses Mama gave him: verse seventeen from Proverbs twenty-one, verses twenty-nine through thirty from Proverbs twenty-three, verse ten from Corinthians I, 6, and verse twelve from Titus 2.

"What did you learn?" Mama quizzed him at the end of the week.

"About lying on the mast of a sailing ship and feeling no pain and God doesn't like drunks." He looked at Mama squarely and said, "Guess he doesn't like Pappy either."

Mama opened her mouth to say something, but swallowed her words and kept her sorrows to herself.

During the rest of Thad's time homebound, he finished reading the Ramsey book Mama had given him and wrote this as his report:

> Dr. Ramsey writes that American colonists became revolutionaries because they were an independent people who pursued liberty in religion and social affairs. They held common

values of simplicity, morality, equal rights, as well as wanting freedom from British rule. He states that slavery is evil and that America needs to stay a unified culture. Too much reliance on English cultural values will dissolve the new nation into many different fragments. He believes that America's strength comes from its federation of states and argues against individual states stressing their independence from the federal union of states.

He also sewed up the sides and the soles of the Ashley boys' boots. Cut and sew. Cut and sew. He worked late each night making other pairs of shoes and boots. But Joshua didn't join him.

"Why isn't he helping me?" he asked his mother one night.

"He goes with me every day to the farm, helping get our house ready for our lodgers."

"But why can't I go too?" he pleaded when the wagon set off one day while Thad was busy making shoes and boots. "I've done all you and Cousin James told me I had to do except earn back twice the money."

"No. Sorry, Thad."

This time Joshua clapped his hands from his perch in the driver's seat of the wagon.

If I didn't have to finish the shoes I've been working on I'd throw one of them right at him. Not going with them felt to Thad more like punishment than memorizing bible verses.

Finally, the end of the second week of his confinement arrived and Thad had earned enough from cobbling to pay back double the amount of money he had misused.

At supper that night, Thad dropped the coins he had earned on the table one by one.

"Count them."

Joshua counted the coins and said, "That's twice what Mr. Ashley paid us for making his sons' boots."

"Now that your debt's been settled, you can move back with us to the farmhouse. Just in time too. The delegates arrive tomorrow. Our beds here will now be available for the delegates who will be staying with cousins Cathy and James," Mama informed Thad.

Thad's heart leapt for joy as he climbed up onto the wagon the next morning and picked up the reins, ready to go back to his farm and Dawn.

"I need you, Thad, to feed and groom our houseguests' horses, besides looking after ours," Mama told him as they rode.

But at that moment all Thad wanted to do was take care of his own horse. He hadn't seen her since she was taken to the farm during his confinement at Cousin James' home.

When the wagon arrived at the farm and stopped in front of their weathered barn, Thad handed the reins to Mama and grasped his cane. He thought he heard whinnying and hooves shuffling.

"Why is Dawn making all that fuss?" he asked.

Mama put her hand on his arm. "Don't rush, Thad. Probably our new lodgers have arrived. See to the feeding and watering of their horses while I greet our guests."

Sure enough Thad saw two new horses in open stalls pawing the ground and snorting. He filled their troughs with feed then looked around for his horse. But Dawn wasn't in the barn. "Wonder where...." No sooner had the words formed in his mouth than he looked up and saw Abner on Dawn. Thad grabbed her reins and rubbed her long neck.

"So good to see you girl. I've missed you."

"Did you miss me too?" Abner responded while climbing down from the saddle.

"Of course," Thad cuffed him lightly with his free hand and gave him his cane. Thad put his good foot in the stirrup and hoisted himself onto the saddle.

"Giddyap girl. Take me to Lookout Mountain!"

Dawn tossed her mane and lifted her head. Horse and rider galloped into a painting of orange and red hues behind stone walls. The breath of freedom filled Thad's nostrils. So good to be back home.

Later, as Thad was leading Dawn into her stall, the piercing blast of Mama's siren sounded, just at the right time as Thad's stomach was making its usual growling noises.

He sat down at the table between a lean man with a bushy beard and another whose big belly touched the table.

"Thad, please meet Mr. Charles Rich from Soreham and Mr. Samuel Shaw from Rutland."

"How-do-you-do," Thad shook hands with each man. "Pleased to meet you."

"This here's a pretty nice farm," Mr. Shaw said to Mama as he passed his pewter dish for her to fill. "I got me a dairy farm up my way. Five young'uns at home to help with the milkin'."

"Abner and I do the milking for my Cousin James," Thad replied.

"Thad gets to be a page at the convention," Abner added.

"I run the post office in Soreham," Mr. Rich said to no one in particular. Turning to Thad he said, "Being a page is sort of like delivering mail, son."

"Which reminds me, Thad," Mama noted, "Cousin Abraham said you're to ride into town with these gentlemen tomorrow morning and take them to the courthouse to meet him there at eight sharp."

"Are you Democratic-Republicans or Federalists?" Thad asked their guests.

"Why us Yankee yeomen are plain folk," Mr. Shaw replied. "We be Democratic-Republicans. Don't take no shine to those aristocratic folk that make up that Federalist Party."

"We believe in the strong rights of states and individuals. Federal government exists to protect the security of the people and maintain our Bill of Rights," Mr. Rich added, "I'm proud of our new postal system, started in Vermont in 1784."

"That's about the same time we came to Danville to live," Mama remembered as she scraped and piled the pewter dishes. The oil lamp threw their shadows against the wall and Thad savored the moment.

Like a colt ready to dash, Thad could hardly wait until tomorrow. *Next best thing to being on this farm will be to meet politicians from all over Vermont. Now I'll have the best of both worlds, at least 'till Mama sells our home and land. But I don't want to think about then. This is now.*

CHAPTER EIGHT

Vermont Assembly in Session

Thad lay awake that night, excitement coursing through his veins. Now that he'd been appointed a page he wouldn't have to endure the shame of his *Devil's Mark*. He could look forward to finding out how his proud new state worked.

Grandpappy had told Thad that it had taken too many years to settle the dispute between Vermont, Connecticut, and New York over land ownership. King George of England had deeded land grants to both New York and Connecticut. Connecticut released their grants to Vermonters but New Yorkers didn't want to turn over their land to Vermont. Grandpappy said that he and his friends were so disgusted with New York they came close to aligning their independent territory to Canada. After fourteen years of negotiations, the New York Assembly finally agreed to sell their land rights if Vermont paid $30,000. *A lot of money for Vermonters to own our own land,* Thad thought.

In 1791 Vermont became the fourteenth state in the United States of America. *Why, my state is only a year older than I am* now.

Thad woke refreshed after sleeping in his own bed. He ate breakfast with their two lodgers and then saddled Dawn to ride with them to the courthouse in town for the start of the Assembly. When they arrived, the main room was filling up with delegates taking their seats. Spittoons stood at the ready. Each table held quill pens and an ink pot. About thirty men milled around the doorway, heads moving from side to side, up and down, hands like visors over their eyes, looking for empty chairs either on the main floor or up in the balcony. They jostled past each other and several men rushed together toward a vacant seat in a race to see who could get there first.

Shouts of "Watch out," "Stop pushing," "Ouch, that's my toe," rose over the other din in the hall. *No wonder. There are not enough desks and chairs,* Thad thought. Some delegates stood against the wall mumbling.

Cousin Abraham cautioned Thad that the real work would start after the formalities of that day's session. "At every session I'll be giving you documents to carry to and from the speaker of the Assembly, Mr. Aaron Leland, and the Governor and his Council, who will be meeting in Uncle Abel's tavern."

Bang, bang! The sound of the gavel striking the high desk at the front of the room reverberated through the huge room and interrupted Thad's thoughts.

"Beginning this day, October 10, 1805, this Vermont legislative session is called to order," Mr. Leland announced.

"Is Mr. Martin Post in the room?"

"Here, Sir." A voice coming from the right side of the room answered.

"Mr. Post, I hereby appoint you clerk of session. Please rise to take your oath. You'll take your seat at that table on the right side of the court-room. Be ready to count the ballots." Mr. Post made his way through the delegates to his place.

Mr. Leland turned his attention to the delegates.

"The first order of business will be the election of our officers and chaplain."

He nodded to Cousin Abraham.

"Mr. Morrill, please come forward to collect the ballots from the clerk and distribute them. I see Mr. William Page, the secretary to the Governor's Council, standing back there."

Thad followed his gaze and saw a man, his hair in a ponytail, standing on the other side of the door.

"Mr. Page, please choose five of your members to help count the ballots."

For most of that morning Thad walked around the hall using his cane for balance, distributing, then collecting ballots, and taking them to the clerk, who with the five council men, counted them. Back and forth. In and around chairs and tables.

Meanwhile, Mr. Leland continued to conduct business. He first asked Mr. Fitch, Congregational minister, to be chaplain. Then he said to Mr. Rich, "I will now take up your resolution to appoint various standing committees to review and discuss the many petitions delegates have brought to this assembly to be considered."

Thad watched Mr. Rich rise and go to stand before the other delegates.

"I need volunteers to serve on the following committees to study the petitions presented to this assembly for consideration during this legislative session: Banks, Roads, Schools, Militia, Taxes, Postal System, Farming, Land Use, and Runaway Slaves." Hands were raised and names were called out as he read off each subject. "Please give your name and choice of committee to our page, who will come around to collect them." He nodded to Thad who hobbled about the room collecting the information requested, moving from one delegate to another. His bad foot scuffled along trying to keep up with his good one. Sometimes the pain became unbearable and he had to sit and take some deep breaths.

After the morning business had been completed and the votes counted, Mr. Leland announced, "Clerk, please rise to read the results of the vote."

Mr. Post collected the paper on his table, cleared his throat, and read, "Mr. Isaac Tichenor, Esq. has been re-elected Governor, Mr. Paul Brigham, Esq., Lt. Governor, and Benjamin Swan, Esq., treasurer. Gentlemen, please rise to take your oaths on the Bible held by Rev. Fitch."

Bang! Bang! The gavel came down again. "The Assembly will recess until two this afternoon when delegates will meet in committees to consider the petitions before us. The Governor and his Council will reconvene at the tavern after the meal prepared there by our local citizens."

Chairs were pushed back, some overturned, cloaks were collected and hats donned as the delegates got ready to recess. Thad's leg hurt from dragging his club foot. His whole body ached from sheer exhaustion. Cousin Abraham put his arm around him.

"Ride with me in my wagon to the tavern for some vittles. You can leave Dawn here," he offered. Thad climbed up on the wagon and succumbed to his weariness. The pain in his leg and foot subsided.

Cousin Abraham flipped the reigns and his horse neighed. The wagon jerked forward and Thad grabbed the side of his seat with one hand and gripped his cane with the other.

"This afternoon," Cousin Abraham advised, "I doubt if there will be many papers to circulate as the delegates and council members will be preoccupied with establishing themselves and considering the way forward. Listen to their deliberations. You may learn something."

As the two of them were hitching the horse and wagon to the post outside the tavern, Uncle Abel rushed out of the tavern, his apron untied and flapping in the breeze.

"You're right on time. I've called on almost every able bodied Morrill to help with the feeding of all these folk. Thad, your mother is here with your brothers in the kitchen, along with Cathy and the other girls and women. Go see what you can do to help. Abraham, will you stand at the door while I make sure our guests are seated?"

Uncle Abel ran back inside the tavern. Thad grasped his cane, limped along behind his uncle and wound his way through the sea of people to the kitchen where the girls were cutting up carrots and peeling potatoes. Mama and Cousin Cathy with Joshua were directing the steady flow of women bringing pots of food. Mama gave Thad the job of filling the delegates' mugs. *Maybe I can sneak one for myself.*

"Don't."

Guess Mama must be a mind reader too.

CHAPTER NINE

Deliberating the Issues

Government by the people was complicated, Thad thought when they returned to the courthouse. He wandered around between the different groups of delegates gathered together and watched them sort through and deliberate the numerous petitions.

One committee considered regulating divorce; another, establishing the boundary between Vermont and Canada; another, an exemption to serving with the state militia; many, on taxes owned by towns; several, whether or not to construct turnpikes and roads around the state. One of the roads being proposed was a road between Danville and the Wells River. *Hey*, Thad thought, *I sometimes ride that way. I can imagine riding Dawn and winding our way through trees and heavy brush to the river. That road is a good idea. Hope it gets approved.*

His ears listened intently to some of the petitions proposed to establish grammar schools. *If one of these proposed schools could be started in Danville, I won't have to continue with Mama and Mrs. Hicks' boring parlor classes.*

Mr. Leland closed the afternoon session around five o'clock and announced that Governor Tichenor would be addressing the opening session the following morning. Thad, exhilarated but exhausted, climbed up onto Dawn and swung his foot over the saddle. Messrs. Shaw and Rich mounted their horses and the two men rode with Thad back to the Stevens' farmhouse.

The next morning rain made the roads muddy so they were late arriving at the courthouse. All the delegates but Mr. Shaw and Mr. Rich were already seated. Mr. Leland was announcing Governor Tichenor. Some of the delegates stood; others remained seated.

"Why doesn't everyone stand?" Thad whispered to Cousin Abraham who was standing in his usual place by the door.

"Because he's a Federalist and most of the delegates here are Democratic-Republicans, like me," he whispered back. "He's not originally from this area, but he did help us get Vermont back from New York, so he became a popular politician. He's a good man, so let's listen to what he has to say."

Thad listened, or at least partly listened, as the Governor praised the agricultural and manufacturing progress of Vermonters. His ears perked up when the Governor talked about an amendment proposed by North Carolina and adopted by Massachusetts to stop the slave trade. He remembered Pappy, before he disappeared, telling Thad that the year he was born the British House of Commons had voted to abolish the slave trade. He then asked Thad why he thought the America still allowed the purchase of slaves. Thad couldn't answer, but maybe the Governor could. He listened more carefully and heard:

"The genius of universal emancipation ought to be cherished by Americans; and that we owe to the character of our country… and the laws of humanity, our best endeavors to repress that impious and immoral traffic."[4]

Cheers arose from the delegates. "Universal suffrage," delegates shouted. "No Slavery!" Thad smiled and joined in the clapping.

He watched the Governor and council members leave the courthouse to reconvene at the tavern. Delegates created yet another committee to prepare an official reply to the Governor's address. That process took up most of the rest of the day. Thad scuttled around the room and listened to the other delegates reviewing and arguing over the submitted petitions and how to present some as resolutions.

In the middle of the afternoon Cousin Abraham sent Thad to the tavern on Dawn. He was to bring back a copy of the North Carolina resolution to amend the United States Constitution, seeking to end the slave trade. The Assembly delegates assigned to write a response to the Governor's proposal needed that copy so that they could write a resolution for Vermont to endorse the abolition of the slave trade. After Thad returned with the document, he hovered near so he could see what they were writing and memorized:

"Universal freedom is one of those fundamental principles of our political institutions which are engraven on the mind, and live in the affections of every true American. And although our country is already infested with slavery, the toleration of which might seem to contravene the general system of our policy, we trust that the humanity and justice of our country will prevent the increase of the deprecated evil, and arrest, as soon as possible, that execrable traffic in human flesh."[5]

Thad's heart beat faster and he stood taller, hoping that not only the Governor but also the rest of the delegates would hear this response and join other states in approving the resolution as a proposed amendment to the Constitution.

Days rolled by. Why does it take so long to pass these resolutions? Then Thad remembered some of Ramsey's thoughts. Americans were independent and each person had an equal right to his opinion. Very rarely did a resolution get passed on its first introduction. Usually petitions were sent back to committee for more deliberation or revisions. New banks received fast approval. So did new roads. But a bill permitting divorce for criminal behavior proposed by Governor Tichenor took days. Chaplain Fitch protested louder than anyone else.

"Marriage is sacred and ordained by God," he preached to the delegates during one of his sermons. "Government should not be setting guidelines for divorce. Only the Bible can do that."

Thad remembered the bible passage since he had to memorize it:

"For the hardness of your heart he (Moses) wrote you this precept (about divorce)"[6]

Could Pappy's drunkenness and disappearance be called "hardness of heart?" Would God allow Mama to divorce him? The Bible mentioned men divorcing wives, not the other way around.

One evening, Thad asked Mama, "Could you divorce Pappy?" She took a long time to reply. Finally, she crossed her arms across her chest and pursed her lips together as she spit out, "I honor my marriage vows. But I wish someday he'd come home sober."

Thad rode back and forth between the tavern and the courthouse with each different version of the divorce resolution. But no version passed. He thought as he rode, *Rev. Fitch's comments must have scared the delegates or maybe they weren't able to define "hardness of heart".*

CHAPTER TEN

The Sickness

Winter winds blew down from Lookout Mountain giving Thad goose bumps. He pulled up the collar of his sheepskin jacket and his cap down over his ears as he prepared to ride Dawn into town. The legislative convention was now in its third week.

Mr. Shaw announced that morning that he wasn't feeling well and couldn't ride with Thad and Mr. Rich. When Mr. Shaw wouldn't eat any of the breakfast Mama served, she placed a hand on his forehead.

"You feel hot. Go back to bed and I'll bring you some honey and apple cider vinegar." Mama's homemade medicines and nursing skills were renowned among Danville families.

Bring me back any resolution from my committee," Mr. Shaw called out as Thad headed to the barn. Mr. Shaw had been serving on the farming committee as his district's dairy farmer representative.

Thad left Mama to tend to her patient and rode with Mr. Rich through the cold wind to the courthouse. About a fifth of the seats were empty. *Maybe more folks than Mr. Shaw were sick,* Thad thought.

He took his place beside Cousin Abraham while Rev. Fitch led the attending delegates in prayer. After the chaplain took his seat, Mr. Leland announced that the President and Fellows of Middlebury College would present a report to the assembled delegates.

"Gentlemen, as you are aware, Middlebury College was incorporated in 1800. From the eight students who enrolled that year, in only five years we have grown to fifty-two students…We are now on a course to provide education equivalent to the best schools in New England. We wish to present to you our present course of study in this document."

Cousin Abraham nudged Thad to take the paper being presented and show it to delegates. While Thad was circulating the document, the President continued,

"In order to maintain an institution of higher learning of quality we ask the assembly to consider a grant for the expansion of our library and the purchase of a telescope for our astronomy department."

Some delegates shook their heads. Mr. Rich asked, "How much will it cost?" The President shrugged his shoulders.

Mr. Jonas Galusha, the chairman of the school committee, rose to speak: "Gentlemen, since no sum has been specified as to the amount of money requested by Middlebury College in their report, and because we have in past years supported them substantially, I request that their petition be held over until next year's General Assembly. I hope by then their President will have provided us with more specific information, including exact costs."

"Here! Here!" Delegates pounded their tables.

Bam went the gavel. "Silence, please. Remember that all committee business needs to be concluded today and resolutions voted on so that they can be sent to the Governor and the Council."

Thad looked up from making the rounds of committee meetings to see Mama talking to Cousin Abraham. *What's she doing here?* He wondered as he made his way to the back of the room where they were standing.

By the time he arrived Mama had already left. Cousin Abraham's brow furrowed as he reached for Thad's arm. "Your mother's gone to your Cousin James' house to check a spotted rash the twins have. Cousin Cathy is also sick. Your mother said to tell you she'd be a while. She asked me if you could get back to the farm early to be with Mr. Shaw and the boys. Joshua's making boots today."

"But…"

"No buts. I'll handle whatever papers need to be taken to the tavern. Now go."

The wind had died down and the sun was shining through the clouds when Thad untied Dawn's reins from around the post and put his foot into the stirrup, throwing his other leg over the saddle. Dawn neighed and they set off once again for the farm.

When they rounded the turn in the road, Thad saw smoke rising from the chimney. *At least Abner and Alanson have kept the fire going. I hope they're not fighting.*

Abner threw his arms around Thad before he'd had a chance to hang his jacket on the peg inside the door. Abner's words rushed out faster than Thad could absorb them.

"Mr. Shaw's upstairs…Alanson's sulking…I put logs on the fire…Mama's gone…Where's Mr. Rich?"

"Whoa. Slow down. I came home because Mama had to go take care of the twins and Cousin Cathy who are sick. Mr. Rich is still at the courthouse.

"I'd better go upstairs to see how Mr. Shaw is doing. Find out what Mama left us to eat for dinner and ask Alanson to set the table."

"How're you feeling?" Thad asked from the foot of the bed where Mr. Shaw was thrashing around.

"Awful," he mumbled through chattering teeth. "Everything hurts. I'm thirsty." Heat radiated from his body. Thad noted that the pitcher on the washstand was almost empty. He dipped a towel hanging by the basin into what little was left, wrung it out and placed it on Mr. Shaw's forehead.

"Abner!" Thad called downstairs. "Bring some water from the pump for Mr. Shaw to drink and to cool down his fever."

After tending to Mr. Shaw's needs, Thad sat down with Abner and Alanson to eat the corn chowder and bread Mama had left for them.

'You goin' help with the milking again?" Abner asked.

"And chop wood?" Alanson added.

"You're hardly ever around and Mama makes us do all the chores."

"All Joshua has to do is cobbling."

"I work as a page," Thad defended.

"What's a page?" Alanson asked.

"A page runs errands for legislators, collecting and delivering papers, and anything else they ask a page to do."

"But you don't have to go to parlor school like we do," Abner whined.

"It's a kind of schooling, listening and learning all about how our government works."

After they'd eaten, Thad checked once again on Mr. Shaw and found him sleeping and snoring.

"Will you wrestle with us, like Pappy used to?" Abner asked. Thad removed his boots to be more agile and put up his hands. "Come get me!" he challenged his two younger brothers, and they came at him, one from in front and one from behind. Thad balanced on one leg and swung his club foot leg to trip them. They both fell to the floor. They kept wrestling until Thad heard wagon wheels squeal.

"Mama…" he began, straightening himself when she came through the door with Joshua.

"What is going on here?"

She put her hands on her hips and looked around the room. Their pewter bowls were still on the table. The fire had gone out and their outer clothes were in a heap where they'd thrown them while they were wrestling.

"Nothing. Just havin' fun, Mama," Alanson spoke with his head down and his hands between his legs.

"Thad. I thought I sent you home to take care of your brothers and Mr. Shaw!" She glared at Thad, put her hand on one hip, and shook her finger. "I've spent all afternoon taking care of sick people and here you've been wrestling all this time."

"He's—or was— sleeping. I gave him a drink and cooled him off."

"I see." Mama turned her back on them and climbed the stairs. Thad heard Mr. Shaw vomiting. He motioned to Abner and Alanson to help him straighten up the mess they'd made. When Mama came back downstairs, she had soiled bedding in her arms.

She gave the bedding to Joshua, sat down in the chair by the fireplace, and sighed. Her arms hung limp at her sides. *She hasn't even commented that the fire has gone out.* Thad beckoned to Abner— pointing first to the fireplace and, then, to the door. Abner motioned to Alanson to follow him and the two boys went out the door to the woodshed.

Mama kicked off her shoes and her eyelids hung half-way down her eyeballs. *She's so tired. I need to do better,* Thad thought.

"Maybe I can look in on some of the sick folk in town after session tomorrow. Save you from coming, Mama."

"I need to go to the cobbler shop tomorrow," Joshua spoke. Thad had been so busy trying to make all things right again, he had forgotten his older brother was in the room.

Mama's eyes were now closed but she managed a faint, "No. I'll go. Thad-- counting on you to help your brothers and see to Mr. Shaw. Maybe after church service...*zzzz.*" She was asleep.

CHAPTER ELEVEN

Nursing Assistant

By Sunday more townsfolk had succumbed to the strange sickness. All of them had splotches of red, high fevers, aches, and chills.

"Probably the dreaded Spotted Fever that comes from ticks in the woods," Mama commented, "although Doc Evans thinks it's more like Measles."

"Did Mr. Shaw get the disease from the animals on his farm?" Thad asked.

"We don't know. We only know that it is spreading."

After Sunday service dinner, with Mr. Rich and Joshua to look after Mr. Shaw and his younger brothers at the farm, Thad went with Mama when she made her rounds visiting the townsfolk who were sick.

"Remember to wash your hands with this lye soap and cover your mouth with this cloth," Mama told him, handing him the soap and cloth. Washing with the soap made his hands as red as those who were sick.

Thad watched Mama greet each sick person and prepare cold compresses to cool down their fever, as Thad had already done for Mr. Shaw. He also helped her change bed linens. She prayed with the sick folks too.

By Monday, the opening day of the last week of the legislative session, Mama had more calls for nursing than she could handle.

"If you want to help, I need you to go with me," she told Thad.

She asked Abraham to allow Thad time off from his page duties in the afternoons and the evenings to help with the nursing of the sick. By now the sickness had depleted the ranks of the delegates. Only half of the seats in the courthouse were now occupied.

"Let the business of this government continue," Mr. Leland announced. "If necessary, for important matters, Thaddeus can obtain the signatures of the bedridden." So not only did Thad have to ride back and forth between the tavern and the courthouse delivering papers to approve and sign but when he visited with sick delegates at the homes where they were staying he needed to ask them to sign documents. He was so busy and so tired he forgot about his lameness.

At each house he visited with Mama he inquired if a delegate was staying with them and if he were sick. Then Mama moved on to minister to the other sick family members, leaving Thad to take care of the sick delegate. After tending to the delegate's needs, Thad asked him if he would be willing to sign the resolutions he'd brought with him.

Of all the resolutions that he carried for signatures, the one concerning the slave trade cessation was the most important the delegates and the council would be asked to approve.

By Wednesday the resolution still needed five more signatures to pass. Thad rode Dawn from house to house, well into the evening, after Mama had returned to their farm. He didn't even take time to eat supper. At the last house he woke up the sick delegate. *I'm not sure he can sign since he shakes so much,* Thad thought.

"Mr. Henry, can you hear me?"

Mr. Henry nodded, opened one eye and gave Thad a glazed stare.

"Would you like some water? May I cool your forehead?"

Thad took the towel and poured water over it into the basin, wrung out the excess, and laid it on Mr. Henry's forehead — pushing back the elder man's white hair. He stared at Thad.

"I remember you from the courthouse," he croaked.

"One more signature is needed to pass the slave trade cessation resolution. Will you be willing to sign?" Thad inquired.

Mr. Henry tried hard to smile through cracked lips and reached for the quill pen. Thad placed one arm behind his shoulders and helped him to a sitting position, laying the paper with the resolution beside him on the bed, close to his shaking hand. Then he dipped the pen into ink and placed it in his hand. Mr. Henry scrawled something on the paper. *I hope that it resembles his signature enough to be accepted.* Mr. Henry sighed and lay back down on the bed saying, "May the good Lord redeem the evil we have done." Then he closed his eyes.

On Thursday Thad handed over the signed document and Mr. Leland announced that the resolution to stop the slave trade had received a majority of yea votes. Fists banged on tables and some delegates threw hats into the air and shouted, "Huzzah!"

That same day the delegates also approved two public grammar schools, one in Orange County and one in Peacham. Thad's countenance fell. Too far away for him. The delegates also appointed Justices of the Peace, naming Cousin Abraham for Danville.

The gathered assembly made one more momentous decision before adjourning. When David Wing, the Secretary of State, suggested that Montpelier be chosen to host the legislative session next year and that town become a permanent seat for the legislature, yeas resounded throughout the room. The assembled delegates also approved a new Capitol Building in Montpelier, to be completed by 1808.

At noon on Friday Mama, Thad and his brothers, along with Cousin Abraham's family and other Morrills who were not sick with fever, sat in the front row of the courthouse to watch Cousin Abraham and the other elected justices take their oaths of office. Thad felt chilled as if someone had left a window open and his stomach was queasy. Mama's eyes looked into his brown ones. She reached over to feel his forehead and said, "Oh, no. Not you too."

Thad's brain muddled everything that happened next: Joshua riding Dawn back to the farmhouse, his being placed in the back of the wagon, his head throbbing with every jolt, puking over the side; then, being half pushed, half carried by Mr. Rich and his brothers up the stairs and into bed. His head spun around and registered a person, who looked like Mr. Shaw, in the next bed.

The red spots came out the next day. Thad remembered recognizing vague faces, feeling cool towels being placed on his head, and asking for water. Most of the time he slept, or thrashed, or moaned, or swore. He thought he heard voices. *Mama's voice saying, "You're not to use that language in this house"* — *Mr. Rich saying, "Good-by"* — *Cousin Abraham asking, "Hello, how're you feeling?"* — *Mr. Swan talking about cows.* He vaguely heard someone sobbing.

Thad almost died. Or so Joshua told him. Some did die. Mr. Henry, whose signature was the last one on the slave trade cessation resolution, died. Worst of all Cousin Cathy died.

"Mama said we're going to move back to Cousin James' home as soon as you're strong enough," Abner told Thad while they were playing checkers on his bed.

"Why?"

"Because Cousin James needs Mama's help now that Cousin Cathy has died."

I hate thinking about living with Cousin James again.

"Got you cornered," he told Abner, not wanting to think about moving.

"You win," Abner conceded.

CHAPTER TWELVE

The Harvest Festival

After many days in bed, Thad's fever finally broke and he felt well enough to join the family for dinner. For his first time out of bed after his fever had broken his club foot hurt more than ever and didn't want to move. Thad had to lean on Mr. Shaw as together they went down the stairs.

"Takes awhile to get your strength back, son," Mr. Shaw said. "T'was a terrible sickness, t'was. Mr. Rich tells me dairy farms didn't get no 'tention in this year's session. My wife writes she needs my 'tention, so's best I be gettin' on home."

They shook hands at the bottom of the stairs. Mama handed Mr. Shaw a sack with food for the long ride home. Mr. Shaw gave her some money. He put on his cloak and hat, said goodbye, and went out the door. *At least he doesn't have the pot belly stomach he came with anymore. Guess that's because the sickness took away our appetites.*

Thad joined Mama and his brothers at the table.

"First, I'll say grace and thank the Lord for Thad's recovery." Mama bowed her head and Thad and his brothers dutifully followed. She passed Thad the soup pot. "Time to put some flesh back on those bones."

"Mama, did you hear that the delegates approved starting a public grammar school in Peacham?"

"No. Guess I was too busy nursing the sick to catch that news. But with me helping to raise James' girls, cook, and taking care of their house, you boys will need to attend an outside school. I won't have time for parlor school. I'll talk to Cousin Abraham and see what we can do about your schooling. At least you and Joshua should attend the new one in Peacham."

"Can we go too, Mama?" Alanson asked.

"We'll see. Now eat your dinner."

Thad really didn't feel hungry yet or, at least, he didn't enjoy eating like he had before. He managed a few bites then put down his spoon. Even though Mama had baked his favorite apple cobbler, it tasted like mush.

Joshua said, "Folks in town are getting ready for the Harvest Festival in two weeks. Every family is being asked to contribute."

Mama sighed, "Seems like we just finished feeding all those delegates. Some folks are still recovering from being sick. We've got to get ourselves moved, and to see to it that Cousin Cathy gets a proper burial— bless her soul— then move us all back to Cousin James' house, and put this farm up for sale again. There isn't enough time left in my days to think about the Harvest Festival."

Thad's stomach refused to accept any more food and he felt like vomiting.

"Can't we keep the farm, Mama, until spring?"

"I'd like to do that, Thad, but since our guests left we have no income coming in and I still have your father's debts to pay off. Besides, the burden for all the outside work falls on Abner and Alanson. They've still got wood to chop and they need their schooling too."

"But can I keep Dawn, please?"

"Well, we can't leave her here with no one to feed her, can we? We'll have to take her along to town with Gerty and Nellie when we move."

At least I can ride back out here once in a while, he thought. He felt his appetite returning.

"Speaking of the Harvest Festival, I guess we could take our apples from the orchard– maybe bake a few pies when I get to town. Boys, after dinner, go gather all the apples you can and put them in the barrel."

Dressed in his Sunday pantaloons and vest, Thad went with Mama and his brothers the next day to attend Cousin Cathy's funeral at Christ Congregational Church. All the pews were filled. Looks like the whole town had assembled. *Either they loved Cousin Cathy's generous spirit or were beholden to Cousin James or Uncle Abel.*

The twins cried and wouldn't let go of Mama's calico dress. The congregation sang "Amazing Grace." Thad glanced over at Cousin James during the service. Cousin James glared back at Thad. His glare felt like a knife being jabbed into Thad's gut while Thad was sure he was thinking, *You should have been the one to die, not her, not my wife.*

As soon as the coffin was lowered into the ground, their Morrill relatives ushered them all back to Cousin James' house. Cousin James sat in Cousin Cathy's favorite rocker by the fireplace with his head in his hands, not really seeing the rest of them. "I can't live without her," he moaned.

Mama placed her hands on his shoulders. "You must— for the twins."

"And you'll have us here so you won't get lonely," she added.

Cousin James' face screwed up into ridges and his eyes blinked to hold in the tears. His hands shook. He whispered, "Thank you, Sarah."

Maybe if he stays this way, he won't notice me anymore. I don't care if anybody notices me.

After eating the food that family and neighbors had brought, talk turned to who was doing what at the Harvest Festival.

"Joshua, you and Thad are in charge of the apple bobbing contest," Uncle Abel announced.

During the following weeks, Thad came and went between their farm and Cousin James' house, wagons taking their belongings trip by trip. For Thad and his brothers there was no time for parlor schooling with Mama taking care of two households. And each of them had chores to do at Cousin James' house, the mill, the carriage house, the barn, the cobbler shop, and their farm. Time went by so fast that when the day for the Harvest Festival arrived, the only reason Thad knew was when he was eating breakfast he noted two apple pies cooling on the window ledge.

"We'll worship first, give thanks, and then go to the tavern. Almost the whole town will be there," Mama announced. "Thad, don't forget the apples and that wash tub."

"How could I forget them," Thad replied with an irritated edge in his voice, "when I helped pick them." *What I don't want to do is be in the midst of that big crowd of people and get jostled around.*

Cousin James sent his icy glare through Thad.

"Enough of your smart tongue! Do as you're told!"

Fortunately, when they arrived at the tavern, Uncle Abel placed the apple bobbing behind the tavern where the bull baiting had taken place. All Joshua and Thad had to do was to fill the tub with water, drop apples into it, and sit by to supervise. Today the weather was unusually warm for November. At least there was no snow.

Abner and Alanson acted as their advance team, mingling with the crowd of townsfolk inside the tavern, calling "See who can get an apple first" or "Bring your favorite girl," and they directed participants to line up outside the back door.

The Morrill twins were first in line, led forward by Mama.

"You have five minutes to bite and capture your apple with your hands behind your back," Joshua told them.

The two girls knelt down on either side of the tub and put their faces close to the water but not in it. Every time they tried to bite into an apple the apple slid away.

"Time's up," Thad said, handing each girl a towel. "Next." The two girls went away without apples.

Thad recognized two of the boys who had bet on the bull with him.

"How're you doin,' Gimpy? Haven't seen you 'round here lately."

"Been busy," he mumbled while Joshua reviewed the rules.

The boys put their faces down into the water and each came up with an apple in his teeth, both soaking wet.

Young and not so young folks kept coming and trying. The boys usually bit the apples right away but the girls were more timid— most not willing to get their hair and dresses wet, except one, a coloured girl. She and an older coloured boy came together. She got her head in the water and grabbed an apple with her teeth before the boy did and stood up— water dripping down her calico dress and apron. She took the apple out of her mouth and smiled at Thad as he handed her a towel. Thad melted. She took the towel from him —her hand lingering in his. Thad blinked.

She blinked back. Thad stared at her as she walked toward the door of the tavern.

"Come on." Joshua woke Thad out of his stupor. "We've got folks waiting."

Abner and Alanson were last in line when the barrel had only a few apples left. The water level in the tub now shallow, Abner and Alanson easily captured the last two apples without even getting wet.

Thad tipped the tub over to pour what was left of the water out, then the four Stevens' brothers joined the others inside the tavern, already seated at long tables, all except the two coloureds who were standing looking like they were not sure whether they belonged. Thad knew about not belonging. Both he and Joshua felt that way with their club feet and being poor. So he encouraged Joshua to go over and ask if the two wanted to sit with their family.

"My name's Joshua and this here is Thad," Joshua said.

"Mine is Lucy and this here is my brother, Festus," the girl replied.

"You live around here?" Thad asked.

"Yes. Nearby on a farm. Our last name is Prince. My grandmama Lucy's visiting us. I'm named after her. My grandpappy — his name was Abijah— he died."

"We're Stevens. My grandparents are Morrills."

Cousin Abraham interrupted any further conversation when he stood and lifted his mug for attention.

"Many of you are aware that at the recent meeting of the General Assembly the delegates did not approve our petition to have a public grammar school here in Danville. Instead, we were approved as the county seat; Peacham, the public grammar school. However, since winter is upon us and the Peacham School in not accessible, we have found a temporary place for a school for our own boys. The Christ Congregational Church on the square has agreed to allow us to have our school in their building as they have recently acquired a new wood-burning stove to keep the building warm this winter. Mrs. Hicks has agreed to be our interim teacher. Classes will begin next week. All boys ten to fifteen years old are invited to attend.

Thad looked over at Lucy. She looked back, swallowed, and shook her head.

What about girls? What about coloureds? Somehow it doesn't seem quite fair.

On the other hand, not only Joshua but also Abner and Alanson could enroll in the new school.

CHAPTER THIRTEEN

School for Boys

"We've got too many chores," Thad complained from his seat at the breakfast table the Monday that the temporary school opened. "When are we going to have time for studying?"

Mama and Cousin James kept them busy from early morning to night. Abner and Thad milked the cows. Joshua and Alanson pumped and carried water. Joshua and Thad worked in the cobbler shop, the carriage house, and groomed the horses. Abner helped out at the mill.

"You'll make time," Cousin James growled.

Mama looked directly at her cousin and boss. She said, "James. The boys' schooling must come first. With them gone half the day, can't we reconsider the chores? Remember what household chores you did before we moved in with you and Cathy. Then you didn't have my boys to haul water, milk cows, groom horses, and work in your businesses."

Thad held his breath, waiting for some sign that their frozen cousin would melt a little. He had a hard time believing that Cousin James was Uncle Abel's son. He didn't act like him at all.

Thad let his breath out cautiously while waiting for the answer.

"I have accounts to keep at the Mill, the carpentry shop, and the lumber yard while running the carriage rental business, Sarah. Now with your family living here I have more mouths to feed. I give your boys a roof over their heads and food to eat. I pay taxes – now apparently raised because of this new school. They need to work for their lodging here. Now if you'll excuse me I have some ledgers to go over."

"Can we get a ride with you to school?" Joshua asked before he was out of the room.

"Maybe you, but the rest of you boys can walk."

"But..." Thad started to object. Mama put her finger against her mouth, silencing Thad.

Now what have I done wrong? I hate him.

"You have Dawn to ride, Thad," she reminded him.

Thad abruptly rose and left the table after Cousin James had left, wanting to get out of that house before he said something he would get punished for. He saddled and rode Dawn so fast he was breathless. He was waiting at the door when Mrs. Hicks arrived to open up the church building for their school.

"Good morning, Thad. Since you're here early, you can help me by bringing in some wood and starting the stove."

Thad sighed. *Must remember tomorrow not to get here before the others.*

As he was collecting the firewood, Zach and Tom rode up with the scraggly- headed skinny boy from the tavern bull fight.

"Looky here," Zach said, "if it isn't Gimpy again." He laughed.

Thad shifted his load of firewood trying to balance himself and control his temper, considering how he might throw the whole pile at Zach and the other two, but thought better of it. He could be the one to fall since he'd left his cane at Cousin James'. If he fell they'd laugh some more and call him other names.

Instead of reacting, Thad said, "Maybe you forgot that my name is Thaddeus. You may call me Thad." He carried the firewood into the church with his club foot shuffling behind. Snide comments and snickering still lingered in the air. The other boys did not offer to help.

"Bulls and bullies bed together," he said loudly as he started the fire in the stove.

"Attention!" Mrs. Hicks shouted hitting her ruler on the edge of the pulpit where she stood. Boys' chatter became low whispers as they searched for their assigned seats in one of the church pews.

As Thad looked around he could see about fifteen boys seated around the large nave of the church. *Didn't seem like a school without desks.*

Between his Morrill cousins and his brothers they made up about three quarters of the students.

"School will now come to order. First, these are the rules you will obey while you're in this building:

1. When you enter the church you will go immediately to your assigned seat.
2. No talking unless your right hand is raised and/or I call upon you to speak.
3. Stand when you speak or recite, and address me as Mrs. Hicks.
4. No fighting.
5. No swearing.
6. You will show respect at all times to other members of the class.
7. Bring your own quill pen, ink pot, and copy book.
8. All books and primers we will study are the property of this school. If you lose or deface any one of them, you must purchase its replacement.
9. Each week I will post assigned chores. You will be expected to know what your chore is for that week.
10. School day will begin at 9 AM and end at 1 PM. There will be one recess. The no fighting rule applies. The tardy bell will be rung at five minutes past nine.

"Any boy disobeying these rules will be disciplined accordingly. On the occasion of your first offense you will feel the sting of this ruler. For your second offense you will sit for an hour on this stool here facing the window. Upon your third offense you will be dismissed for the day; and your fourth offense will result in your being expelled."

Thad hadn't brought any quill pen, ink, or copy book. Probably Mama gave them out after he left the house. He looked over at Joshua, Abner, and Alanson. They seemed to be well supplied, but not him.

"Today, I will be determining your level of learning. Some of you I've taught in my parlor," Mrs. Hicks said, looking over at Thad and Joshua.

At least I've memorized most of what she taught in the past. This will be easy.

Half way through the morning, after each boy in the room had been quizzed by Mrs. Hicks, she announced a twenty minute recess.

Thad slid down the pew toward the aisle and stood up, with his hand on the pew in front to balance his weight. Zach came by and pushed him back down with a challenge. "Race you to the door," Zach said grinning.

"The tortoise usually beats the hare," Thad replied, standing up again and plodding toward the door while seething inside.

I can beat him up, he thought, and then he remembered the "no fighting" rule. He took his time walking down the aisle of the church. By the time he had made his way to the door of the church, Mrs. Hicks was standing outside ready to ring the end of recess bell so he ambled back to his assigned pew and seat.

"You're late," Mrs. Hicks snapped at the last person to take his seat. She hit him on the hand with her ruler.

Thad mouthed, beat you, while Zach nurtured a stinging hand.

From then on Thad didn't get any more bullying. But he and Zach were not exactly friends. Thad couldn't trust that their truce would last so he didn't join the other boys at recess.

After the first school week had ended, Mrs. Hicks assigned Thad to the most advanced class of students. However, he had very little time during the school day to study the arithmetic and Latin books she gave him since she also assigned him to tutor the younger boys on their multiplication tables.

CHAPTER FOURTEEN

The Fugitives

White swirls of snow rested on Dawn's mane. Mist from her breathing mingled with Thad's own breath as they rode to the town post office after class.

Abner and Alanson were walking and Joshua was still waiting for Cousin James to come by the church to take him home. Mama had asked Thad before he left that morning to check at the post office to fetch their mail. With the Latin book tucked away in his saddlebag to keep it dry, Thad rode slowly through the first new snow thinking about school.

Suddenly Dawn whinnied and jerked at her reins. "What's wrong, girl?" Thad said, patting her neck. Two dark figures dashed across their path and disappeared into the space between the post office building and the general store. Thad tied Dawn's reins to the hitching post, hobbled into the post office building, and asked for the Stevens' mail.

"Nothing today," the postmaster answered. "But I do have several items here for your Cousin James. Looks like some bills. Here, you can take them to him." He handed the tied buddle to Thad.

Thad scrunched the envelopes down into his saddlebag on top of his Latin book. As he was about to step into the stirrup to mount Dawn he felt a tap on his shoulder and a voice whispered,

"Ple-a-se, Mass'r."

He turned around to see pleading dark eyes on a boy his same height.

The boy's teeth were chattering and his body shaking in its thin shirt and torn pants. The falling snow whitened the black toes sticking out from where the top and soles of his shoes met.

"Claude and me, we'se lost our de-rection. Those men with guns, they'se after us."

"What men with guns?"

"The slave hunters."

"But we've no slaves here in Vermont."

"They's been chasin' us all the ways from Boston. We been followin' de-rections to Canada but we done got lost." His teeth chattered again. With his arms crossed he rubbed his shoulders and stomped his feet.

"We need to get you someplace warm," Thad replied. And some decent winter clothes. "Where's Claude? And what's your name?"

"Name's Jim. Claude's over there, try'n to get warm." He pointed to the space between the buildings.

"That you, Thad?" a female voice asked." Nice horse."

"What? Who? Where?" Thad turned back to Dawn and saw a girl, whose face was hidden in a hood pulled over her head, patting Dawn's nose. She pulled back her hood, revealing a head of long black curly hair. Thad recognized her, that face and smile he'd remember anywhere.

"Lucy!" He stared at her until he sensed the cold, shivering boy was still standing behind him.

"You've come in time to help me figure out where we can find a dry, warm place for Jim, here, and his friend, Claude. They're lost and the bounty hunters are after them."

Lucy lifted her head then stepped back from Dawn so she could see Jim, and her smile disappeared.

"Oh. We do need to get them out of this cold. Festus and I brought our hay wagon into town. They can ride with us— but where to?"

"I'm on my way back to Cousin James' where my brothers and I are living now. He owns the grist mill and has a carriage house and barn where our cobbler shop is."

"Won't the slave hunters find them there?" Lucy asked. "They usually visit all the houses in a town first."

"We'll think of something."

"I'll ask my brother if he can bring the wagon over here."

Thad put his coat around Jim and together they went to look for his friend, Claude. In the space between the store and the post office they found Claude sitting with his back to one wall of the building, his knees pulled up to his chest, his long arms circling them, and his head burrowing into them. Jim placed his fingers to Claude's mouth to attempt to quiet his teeth from their loud chattering.

"The good Lord done help us onc't agin toward freedom," Jim spoke comforting words.

Lucy, Festus, and Thad covered Jim and Claude with hay. The falling snow made a white blanket on top. Thad mounted Dawn and followed the wagon to Cousin James' – excitement and fear churning in his stomach as he faced either his wrath or acceptance of two runaway slaves staying in his home. Mama opened the door.

"No mail for us, Mama. Some letters came for Cousin James, though." Thad paused, and then continued, "Got some visitors outside."

"Well, don't just stand there. Invite them inside where it's warm. And shake the snow off before you come any further." Thad beckoned to Lucy and Festus who uncovered the two runaways. The four of them followed Thad through the door, dusting off the snow and shuffling their feet as they did so. Abner and Alanson and the twins crowded around, their eyes wide and inquisitive.

"Mama, remember Lucy and Festus from the Harvest Festival? These other two are Jim and Claude, running away from bounty hunters who've been following them from Boston."

"You boys must be cold and hungry. Come over here by the fire and get warm. Then we'll find you some dry warm clothes. Thad, go fetch some winter clothes that belong to you or Joshua that might fit these brave young lads."

Thad picked up his cane and was making his way up the stairs with it when he felt a blast of cold air on his back. In walked Cousin James and Joshua.

"What are these coloureds doing here in my home?" Cousin James shouted.

Lucy and Festus moved back against the wall behind the open door. Jim and Claude moved away from the fire and went to join them. Thad stopped, turned around, and headed back down the stairs.

Mama said, "James. I invited these sojourners to warm themselves by our fire. They're runaway slaves who Thad met on his way home from school. You've already met Lucy and Festus at the Harvest Festival. They helped bring these cold and starving boys here. The Bible says…"

"I don't care what the Bible says," Cousin James interrupted. "I'm not harboring any runaway slaves here in this house. I'm not risking my reputation as a leading businessman in this town."

Mama stood, her arms stiffly pressed against her sides, and glared at Cousin James.

"The Bible says to feed and clothe them, James. I'm going to do both. Then we'll decide where they can stay."

Right then and there, Mama became Thad's friend for life.

"I want these coloureds out of my home when I come back from the mill," Cousin James spit out. He went back out the door toward the carriage house, slamming the door behind him.

Thad looked toward Mama, now clearing the table, then to Lucy, who shrugged her shoulders and turned her head away from the door. Meanwhile, Jim and Claude went upstairs with Thad and came back down wearing pantaloons, stockings, and flannel vests that Thad retrieved for them. Thad never liked his pantaloons, even though all the other boys wore them.

"Mighty fine chicken and corn fritters, Ma'am. Reminds me of my Mammy's," Jim said after eating the food Mama had prepared.

"Where is your Mother?" Mama asked.

"Last I knows, she in Virginny. Farmer done bought me, pulled me by rope and kept beating me to move faster. One night, I done run. Could hear them dogs followin.' Met Claude in the woods — he knows the route to follow — memorized it from quilts. We been running together ever since. Last conductor gave us de-rections to station master Johnson's safe house in Peacham, it being our last station 'afore Canada. Think we must have missed it. Didn't think we'd make it — that is 'til we met Mr. Thad, Lucy, and Festus here."

"You must have missed Peacham. It's about seven miles south of here," Mama replied. "We'll take you back there."

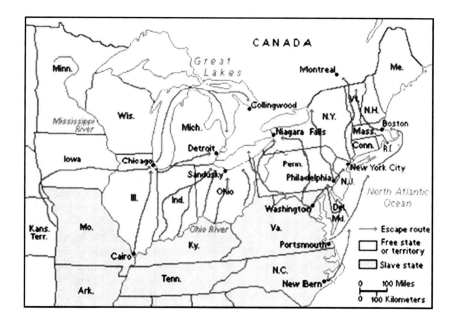

CHAPTER FIFTEEN

Hatching a Plan

"We'll need a plan," Thad spoke first.

"They need new shoes," Joshua spoke second.

Mama frowned. "That will take so long that you won't be gone when James returns. Thad, they have to be out of here when he returns."

Lucy spoke next. "They can come with Festus and me. We live on a farm outside of town— difficult for slave catchers to find since no road runs by our land."

Festus shook his head. "No, Sister. The first place them slave hunters will look is with us freed blacks. Remember, they knows where we live." He shuttered. "They almost carted me off onc't thinkin' I was a runaway. Fortunately Grandmama knew the law in these parts."

"There's an open stall in the barn," Thad reminded them. "They can hide and sleep there while we make their shoes."

"And we can bring them food," Susan piped up.

"As long as Cousin James doesn't find out," Abner added.

"Or them slave hunters don't come 'round," Festus reminded everyone.

"I can stop at the general store or the post office every day on my way home from school and ask around so we can be warned if they do come," Thad said.

"Meanwhile we need to start on their shoes— probably best to make boots, this time of year," Joshua concluded.

Lucy looked outside. Even though white flakes of snow were still visible through the window, the snow had not accumulated much on the ground.

"And best we be getting back home 'afore the snow gets too deep. If the road's not too bad, I'll ride back into town tomorrow and we can figure out how to get Jim and Claude to their next station in Peacham." She opened the door to leave and the others followed.

Mama said, "Here, boys, take some warm blankets with you, and make up a bed for Jim and Claude in the open stall. These sweaters and scarves should help too."

"Ah… choo!" Jim sneezed.

"And better take this honey/vinegar drink," Mama added. "Won't do for either one of you to get sick now you've come this far."

"Thank you, Ma'am. You Northerners' mighty kind."

Thad motioned to Abner to help carry all the items Mama was now thrusting upon him. He was puzzled about where she found all the extra blankets until he remembered that they had brought extra bedding with them when they left the farm.

Once more Thad found himself doing the cobbling, but this time he didn't mind as he was helping Jim and Claude. Besides, he had a new friend in Lucy and hoped she'd returned home safely. He imagined her wagon rumbling over rutty roads and then their horse crashing through the underbrush to get to their farmhouse. These visions flashed through his head as he chose the lasts to make new boots for Jim and Claude. Fortunately they had enough leather left over from their past few jobs.

Jim and Claude watched and asked questions about procedures. *They'll make fine cobblers someday,* Thad thought, *if they ever get to Canada.* He vowed to keep them safe until they got to Mr. Johnson's safe house.

Abner and Alanson appeared at the door, "I see him… Cousin James! He's coming near."

"Go meet him and offer to take care of his horse and buggy for him, Abner. Alanson, show Jim and Claude where the open stall is and move over the feeding trough to block the stall door. Then go back and occupy the twins so they don't tell their father where the boys are hiding."

Thad was counting on Cousin James liking to have one of them do all his chores for him. He figured it right because he heard him say to Abner, "Thank you kindly." Then Thad heard his footsteps move back toward the house. Before long he heard the clip, clop of a horse's hooves coming toward the barn and Abner's voice saying "Good boy." Thad breathed deeply now he knew that the runaways would be safe for that night at least. But he was still concerned the twins might tell where the two runaways were hiding.

"Joshua, how can we make sure they don't tell?"

"I don't know. Girls love to tell secrets."

"How can we trust they don't tell their father?" Abner asked, poking his head around the corner.

"Susan and Catherine want to bring Jim and Claude food. I'll make up a story about a secret society they can only join if they promise not to tell."

"Good strategy, Abner, let's hope it works."

The three of them went into the parlor and interrupted a checkers game that Alanson and the twins were playing.

"We have a club that only we Stevens can belong to," Abner put his finger on his lips and shook his head.

"But we want to join too. May we?" Susan said, jumping up and down.

"Well," Abner looked at Thad and winked. "Only if you can pass certain tests since the club is a secret society and if you tell, even your pappy, you can't join."

Both Susan and Catherine nodded and put their own fingers over their lips. "We won't tell."

"There are two tests you have to pass to enter the club," Abner said with great solemnity.

"What are they?" Catherine asked.

"Here's the first one: When you clear the dishes from the table tonight, you're to put a plate with food on it and give it to Thad, without your father seeing you do it. If you pass that test, Thad will give you the next test."

Now what's Abner up to? I have no idea what second test he's thinking about. Besides, I think Susan and Catherine are afraid of me. I answer them in monosyllables when they ask me questions and scowl at them. They avoid me when they see me coming.

"But...," Susan started to say, her lower lip trembling.

"It's all right, Susan." Thad forced a smile.

At supper, Thad's brothers kept up a lively conversation— not letting the girls find a way in to say anything. Susan got an extra pewter plate from the cupboard and when Mama was dishing out food, she hid one in her lap.

Joshua engaged Cousin James in conversation. "Had us some new customers this afternoon at our cobbler shop. We'll need to work on the order after supper so's to have them ready by tomorrow."

Susan held out her second plate to be filled while Mama was looking at Joshua and saying, "What about your school work?"

"Cousin Sarah, you forgot me."

Mama absentmindedly gave Susan the food.

Has she forgotten? Thad realized that they hadn't involved Mama in their plan to keep the twins from telling. *Tarnation!*

Susan slipped the plate under the table into Thad's lap opposite where she was sitting.

When Mama announced that the time had come for dessert, she asked Susan and Catherine to clear the table and then give out the apple pie slices on other pewter plates.

Thad said, "I'll take my Latin book and join Joshua in the cobbler shop. Susan, you can clear this plate, as I've eaten all I want." He handed Susan the plate he had eaten off and reached down to put the other plate with food on it into the saddle bag at his feet.

"Same here, can you clear my plate as well?" Joshua added.

"Me too," said Abner and Alanson in unison. All of them had left un-eaten food on their plates.

Mama said, "What's the matter with your supper? Aren't you hungry? Don't you like....." Then, as if lightening had struck her brain, finished with .....Oh."

Cousin James said, "Well, I like the supper you prepared, Sarah. I'll take my pie with my tea in the parlor."

"Mama, we'll need the candles," Thad whispered.

"I'll bring them, Thad," she whispered back. By this time she had caught on. She scraped the remaining food on empty plates, handed them to Abner and Alanson, and grinned at them all.

As soon as Thad, his brothers and the twins had seen for themselves that Jim and Claude were comfortable and well fed, Thad gave Susan and Catherine their next test.

"When your father leaves to drop off Joshua at school tomorrow, you're to come over here to fetch Jim and Claude to come to the house for breakfast. The rest of the morning watch out for any strange persons you see or your father's buggy returning. In either case Jim and Claude will need to go back to their hiding place in the barn."

Mama put her arms around the two girls when they returned. "We'll do it together and keep it a secret, won't we girls?"

"Then can we join the Stevens' club?" Susan asked.

"Maybe we'll rename the club the Stevens-Morrill Secret Society," Mama laughed.

First time I've heard her laugh since Pappy left.

CHAPTER SIXTEEN

A Narrow Escape

School drags today. Wish the dismissal bell would ring. Wonder if I'll see Lucy after class. I get the ruler slap once because I didn't answer a question Mrs. Hicks asked me. I get to sit on the stool with my back to the class because I answered a question she asked someone else; I answered without raising my hand. Don't know why I can't say what the answer is when I know it, which I usually do. Finally, clang, clang…

Thad grabbed his jacket and made fast time to the door. He hopped with one foot, slip-slid the other behind him. Abner and Alanson came out the door as he was mounting Dawn. Abner pointed to the post office building.

"What are those two men doing?"

Thad looked over in the direction they were pointing and saw two strange men hitching their horses to a post.

"Hurry," he said to Abner and Alanson. "Run over there and wait for me. See what they're up to. I'll follow on Dawn."

When Thad entered the post office, the two men were talking to Postmaster Adams.

"Seen either of these Negroes in this here town?"

These must be the two slave hunters after Jim and Claude.

One of the men held up two papers.

Postmaster Adams studied the sketches on the papers. "Don't rightly know. Now let me think." He rubbed his goatee.

Thad's heart skipped some beats as he waited for Postmaster Adams to respond. *What if Postmaster Adams recognizes the sketches? Maybe Jim and Claude were inside the post office before I saw them outside.*

"One coloured family, a boy and a girl, sometimes comes in here. Oh, here she comes now."

Thad turned around and saw Lucy coming in the door.

The two men walked up to her and each grabbed one of her arms.

"Okay, nigger-girl, where'd you come from?"

One of the men shoved the sketches under Lucy's nose.

"You with these two runaways?"

Thad reached out and knocked the papers out of the man's hand.

"Don't you dare speak to her like that! She's no runaway slave."

The other man let go of Lucy and grabbed Thad's arm and his saddle bag fell to the floor.

"So I've caught you nigger-lover-boy! You can't run with that Devil's Foot, now can you?" he sneered. "Maybe you know them runaways."

A crowd gathered. Thad wrestled his arm free from the man's grip and leaned over to pick up his saddle bag. Abner and Alanson bent down at the same time and their heads met. "Run home," Thad mouthed, "and warn them."

Postmaster Adams came out from behind his window. "This girl's not a runaway. Her family's lived here for years. We're a free state."

"Well, federal law says we have a right to collect other folks' property who done run away even in your free state. So we'll go door to door and find out if any of you are harboring these fugitives." The man pointed a finger at each person in the gathering crowd of onlookers.

Abner and Alanson melded into the crowd and Thad watched as they slipped out the door behind the two men.

"Starting with your house, sonny-boy." One of the men gripped Thad's arm again and shoved him to the door.

"I've come from school to check our mail," Thad protested, looking over at Postmaster Adams who went behind the window again.

"Let me see…sorry, nothing for you today," Postmaster Adams said from behind the window.

"Okay. Both of you are coming with us," the other man ordered.

Thad glanced over to see Lucy, her eyes were wide open, trying to say something, but couldn't seem to get the words out.

"She rode her horse…hitched outside," Thad said for her.

"All right. You can ride your horses, but we'll be riding right beside you. See, we've got our pistols cocked, so don't try to get away," one of them said.

Thad mounted first. Lucy followed, sitting side saddle on her horse. Holding onto their pistols with one hand and the reigns with the other, the two slave hunters mounted their horses. They rode beside Lucy and Thad's horses—— keeping close.

Remembering that Jim and Claude were in the house and needed to hide, Thad kept a tight rein on Dawn so she'd walk, not trot. Lucy picked up the cue and did the same.

"I think my horse is lame," she said loudly.

"Well, girlie, one of the men says, "you can always ride behind me with your cute ass next to mine."

"No she can't!" Thad said through clenched teeth.

"Watch your fat lip, nigger-lover. You're in trouble already for interfering with the law."

Thad kept a wary eye out for any attempt the men might make to force Lucy off her horse.

They walked their horses through town.

"That's where I live," Thad said, pointing out Cousin James' house in the distance to the two men.

Uh, oh! Cousin James' buggy was out in front. Hope Abner and Alanson got there in time to warn Jim and Claude.

"In case the fugitives are in there and you try and warn them, we've got these pistols on your heads so don't try anything."

One man grabbed Lucy's arm and the other, Thad's. Mama opened the door, stared at the men holding pistols to the children's heads, and with her hands on her hips said to them, "What's the meaning of this?" and "Who are you anyway?"

Cousin James, who had been seated eating at the table stood up and walked over to the door.

"Are you Sheriff's deputies? Haven't seen you around here before."

The two men put their pistols back in their holsters.

"Sorry to bother you good people but we're searching every house here in this town for two runaway slaves believed to be hiding somewhere near."

"No runaway slaves here," Cousin James said. "They were here yesterday but I sent them away. I'm a law abiding citizen."

Right then Thad wanted to wrestle him to the ground and gag his mouth.

"Do you know where they went?" asked one of the men.

"No. But maybe Thad knows where they are. He brought them here."

"Ah. Hah! I thought so. Maybe with a good beating he'll tell us."

"But you can't do that!" Mama cried, reaching out her hands to block the two men from making any advances toward Thad. Then, slowly, she lowered her arms and spoke calmly. "One of my cousins is the Justice of the Peace around here. He doesn't approve abusing children. He'll send the sheriff to lock you up if you so much as touch a hair of my son's head."

The men backed off. "Mind if we look around?"

"Not a bit," Mama said with a forced grimace. "If you don't mind if we finish our dinner. But you must be hungry too, so why don't you sit down and join us?" She turned and pointed to the table where Cousin James now had resumed eating.

"Much obliged," one of them responded. "Mighty kind of you Ma'am, since we'se been a' traveling."

Mama turned to Abner and Alanson and picked up a plate off the table. "You boys please take this plate out to Joshua. He said he had to finish an order for boots today." Abner and Alanson rose from the bench where they were sitting. Abner mumbled, "We'll take our plates too and finish eating in the cobbler shop."

"Gentlemen, here, please take my boys' empty seats."

The two slave hunters sat down at the table, their backs to the door.

Abner gave Thad a nod as he headed for the door. Meanwhile Mama was busy filling new plates for the two slave hunters while talking to them. Susan and Catherine stopped eating, their eyes practically popping out of their heads. They stared at Lucy and Thad standing by the door. Thad looked at them directly and put his fingers to his lips and shook his head. Abner and Alanson came and stood in front of Lucy and Thad so that they were hidden from view. Thad opened the door and the four of them slipped out.

"I've got an idea, "Lucy said after they closed the door.

"First, let's bring our horses into the barn," Thad replied.

Meanwhile, Alanson kept up a running dialogue.

"We ran all the way here…got home before Cousin James…Mama shooed Jim and Claude to the barn…rearranged the table settings… Cousin James came home with Joshua … he said he had to finish an order to send out dinner. We had just sat down at the table when you arrived. What'll we do now?"

"We'll see to Jim and Claude. Abner, go see how Joshua is coming along with those boots. Where's the small Conestoga wagon?"

"It's here," Alanson said, pointing to the old covered wagon in the large barn that had been in the Morrill family for years.

"Lucy, do you think you can hitch up your horse to the wagon along with the draft horse and get Jim and Claude out of here?" Thad asked her.

"Sure," she said and went to hitch up the horses.

Thad found Jim and Claude and hid them inside the covered wagon with the blankets and sweaters Mama had provided. Joshua threw in their finished boots.

"Joshua, will you go inside with Abner and Alanson and keep those slave hunters occupied? If they ask where we are, tell them that we had to see to Lucy's lame horse. Meanwhile we'll take Jim and Claude where they will be safe.

Oh, and when those men and Cousin James leave, ask Mama to bring us directions to the Johnson safe house in Peacham. Tell her she'll find us where the meadow meets the mountain. She'll know where that is."

Thad's brothers returned to the house. Lucy drove the wagon and Thad rode on Dawn alongside, his body tense and his heart pounding, hoping that Cousin James and the slave hunters would not see or hear them. He only began to relax when they rounded the corner and lost sight of Cousin James'.

CHAPTER SEVENTEEN

Rescued

No one in town paid any mind to the wagon with its precious cargo. After they passed the outskirts of the town, they rode silently by trees standing like bare-limbed sentries among the evergreens. When the Stevens' farm came in sight, Dawn strained forward ready to get to her familiar barn.

"Meet you at the farm," Thad shouted to Lucy as Dawn cantered ahead.

Dawn neighed and shook her head up and down as if to say, "Yes! I'm home." Thad led her into her old stall in the barn. Then he went to collect logs and kindling to start the fire.

"We're here," Lucy called. Thad looked over his shoulder to see two black heads appear from under the canopy of the covered wagon that had halted before the barn.

After collecting firewood, Thad reached under the feeding trough and found the key Mama had hidden there when they moved. Once inside the farmhouse the four of them worked together to build a fire in the open hearth.

"Think they'll come here 'alookin" for us?" Claude asked.

"Not 'till they search the other houses in town and our farm," Lucy replied.

I'm not so sure. If we don't return with Lucy's horse, while the bounty hunters are still at Cousin James'. If the twins don't squeal. If Cousin James doesn't send out a posse to find us. Too many ifs for my comfort. Fear lodged itself in the back of Thad's brain like a throbbing sore.

"Do you have anything to eat?" Lucy interrupted his thoughts.

"Yes," His responded. "We store potatoes, apples, turnips, carrots, cabbage and preserves from our garden in our root cellar."

But the double doors to the cellar were padlocked. Thad assumed Mama had the key.

"What do we do now?" Jim asked.

Thad pondered his question. After processing options, he replied, "Sometimes when Mama loses a key she gets the blacksmith to open the door and then has him make a new one or buys a new padlock. I'll go find him. I'll tell him Mama lost her key again.

You three go inside and keep the fire going so you can stay warm. If you see the slave hunters heading this way, douse the fire and head into the woods."

"How will we know if it's safe to come back?" Lucy asked.

"We'll have a special signal. Mama keeps a siren in the barn. She uses it to call us in from the fields. If I get back and you're not here, I'll make three blasts on the siren."

"Hurry back. I'se still hungry," Jim added.

Thad knew where Mr. Worth, the local blacksmith, lived so he flew like the wind to reach his place and found the smithy at his forge.

"I've got a problem, Mr. Worth. Need your help opening a padlock"

Mr. Worth pushed back his eye protector mask and looked at Thad inquisitively. "I thought you and your Mama had moved into town?"

Thad breathed deeply and calculated his response. "We did, but Mama asked me to ride out here to get some food from our farm's root cellar. She forgot to give me the key or lost it. I don't want to ride all the way back to town to see if she has it."

"Well….guess I could ride back with you. Let me get my tools. I'll need to break the lock, if'n you don't have the key."

Since Thad wasn't sure Mama would want him to break the padlock, he asked Mr. Worth, "Could you possibly open it without breaking it?"

"Maybe," he mumbled, mounting his horse.

They rode side by side back to the farmhouse. When they arrived, Thad saw Mama climbing down from Cousin James' buggy. *Is Cousin*

James here poking around? Where are Lucy, Jim, and Claude? Then he remembered about asking her to bring the directions.

"Mama!" Knowing that Mr. Worth was beside him, Thad added, "Did you bring the key to open the padlock? I couldn't open the doors to the root cellar to get the food you wanted since you forgot to give me the key, so I went to find Mr. Worth."

"What?" she said, her eyebrows raised and her mouth in a big O.

"Remember, I don't have the key to open the root cellar because of all the mouths you need to feed at Cousin James'. Is he here too?" Thad jerked his head in the direction of the farmhouse, hoping she'd pick up the clue and get his double message.

"No. But he let me borrow the buggy. Thought you'd need help bringing back what I wanted."

"Oh...." Mama paused, and then added, "Thought I told you, Thad, where to find the key to the padlock. Guess I forgot."

"Then you won't be needing me," Mr. Worth said.

"Sorry to have troubled you, Mr. Worth. Much obliged that you came, though. I think we can manage."

After Mr. Worth was out of range so he couldn't hear them talk, Thad sighed and explained. "We were hungry, Mama, and I couldn't open the padlock to the root cellar. But before you open it, let me see if Lucy, Jim, and Claude are still inside the house. They may have run into the woods when they saw the buggy as I told them to."

"We really don't have time to cook a meal," Mama said "I have to have the buggy back when Cousin James comes home from the mill. I told him I needed to come back to our farmhouse to get some supplies from the root cellar, so we were thinking alike. However, we don't want Cousin James to find out that his wagon is missing. I did bring some food along with me with the directions to the Johnson station in Peacham — but not the key. That's hidden under a rock near the entrance to the root cellar.

I left as soon as those men finished searching the house and the barn. They were mad when they found out that you and Lucy had gotten away. They said they would return after they searched the other houses in the village and Lucy's farm. They think you've gone there with the runaway slaves."

Mama told Thad all this as they found the key, opened the double doors to the root cellar, and began loading up the wagon and buggy.

"Lucy! Jim!" Thad called. No answer. As he suspected. They were in the woods.

"Oh. No!" Mama cried.

"I'll wind up the siren while you finish loading," Thad called to her as he headed for the barn to find the old siren.

Blaw! Blaw! Blaw! Its blaring sound carried out into the meadow. Three black figures emerged from the trees.

"We ran when we saw the buggy— thought it was your Cousin James. I know he doesn't like us. Is he gone?" Lucy asked.

"No. Mama came in the buggy alone and she brought some food. She's going to drive Jim and Claude in the wagon to Mr. Johnson's safe house in Peacham. Lucy, you can ride your horse beside the wagon."

"I best be getting' home," she said.

"Not a good idea. The slave hunters think we've gone there. Stay at Mr. Johnson's for a while," Thad pleaded.

"I'm not afraid and my Mammy's expectin' me."

"But I am afraid. They're bad men and I don't want you to get hurt"

"Thad. We're used to being hurt. My Pa will know what to say if they show up."

"Hurry up, Thad. We need to get moving," Mama called from where she was finishing piling potatoes, turnips, carrots, and jars of preserves into the wagon.

"Leave room for Jim and Claude, Mama!" Thad reminded her.

Thad went back into their farmhouse to make sure no dangerous red embers were lingering in the fireplace, then locked the door, and hid the key. When Thad come out, Lucy had already mounted her horse and Mama had hitched Dawn to the wagon. Thad left to take the buggy back to Cousin James'.

He watched Lucy as she trotted on her horse down the road. Anxiety gripped his body. Thad had forgotten to ask her how he could find her farm.

CHAPTER EIGHTEEN

Overcoming Troubles

Fooling Cousin James had been easy up until now. What would happen if he found out? Thad wondered on his ride back to town. He really didn't want to be around him any more than he had to at meal times.

"Are we in the club, Thad?" Susan asked as soon as Thad opened the door.

"Depends." Thad peered over her head and saw Abner nodding.

"We didn't tell the secret and we passed the tests. Abner said that you would tell us if we're in when you got back." Catherine jumped up and down in front of Thad.

"Please!"

Thad put his hand on her head and bent down to whisper, "Only one more test. Bring me my cane over there against the wall and you're in." Both girls ran at once. Catherine retrieved Thad's cane first.

The twins were turning out all right after all.

"Thank you. Welcome to the Stevens-Morrill Secret Society."

Thad bowed first to girls and then with a swish of his hand, he bowed to Abner. "The buggy is at your service to escort Sir James Morrill, owner of the Danville Mill, back to his abode."

"Can we come?" the girls said in unison.

"Guess so, if you don't mind being squeezed," Abner said.

When they returned, Cousin James asked, "Where's your mother? I gave her the buggy to bring back some food from your root cellar. Why isn't she here?"

Thad froze. "Ah…Ah." Think fast. "She…"

Joshua came to his rescue, "Cousin Abraham came for her—— said it was an emergency."

"We get to serve the beans and brown bread," Catherine said as she passed out the pewter dishes and spoons.

After they were all seated around the table, Cousin James asked Thad, "Did you and that coloured girl get her horse taken care of?"

"Yes," Thad responded. "And she went home."

"Humph. Well you're still in trouble with those men who were here. You shouldn't have interfered."

"I know. But they were nasty."

"Be that as it may, the law is the law. Your Cousin Abraham will tell you that. I don't want any more trouble, do you hear me?" If looks could kill, his would have.

Trouble is one thing Thad didn't want either, but one had to take risks to do what was right. And it was right to help Jim and Claude escape to freedom, and his feelings about Lucy were right. But no use in telling that to Cousin James.

"Yes, Sir."

Thad certainly didn't want any more trouble at school either. So he tried to keep calm when other boys started their bullying tactics again. He planned each day to take his time getting ready for recess so that he would be there to open the door to go outside when the bell was about to ring. This routine kept him safe.

After school had been in session for a month and the cold and snowy weather made going outside for recess impossible, Mrs. Hicks announced to the students that during recess they would be memorizing lines from William Shakespeare's play Hamlet, preparing to perform for their parents.

Thad was memorizing his lines.

"To be, or not to be, that is the question: Whether 'tis nobler in the mind to suffer the slings and arrows of outrageous fortune or to take arms against a sea of troubles."

When Zach whispered in his ear, "Want to meet us at the tavern after school tomorrow?"

Instead of picking on me, they're asking me to join them? Do I trust the invitation or are they only out to trip me? Would I be permitted to go to the tavern after what happened before? But that was before the assembly when I spent lots of time there because of being a page. Mama didn't object then. Maybe Zach and the other boys were getting used to seeing me limp. Maybe they invited me because I'm the smartest in the school. These ponderings went through Thad's head before he said,

"Sure."

"Bring a ton of rocks," Zach told him.

What does he mean? The only rocks I know border the pasture on our farm. Then he remembered that rocks meant money. But I don't have any money. All the money we make cobbling goes to Mama to keep to help pay off Pappy's debts. Cousin James certainly doesn't give us any money, although he has plenty of it.

On his way home Thad considered his options. *Could I ask Mama to lend me some money saying that I had to buy a special book for school? But she'd probably go and ask Mrs. Hicks about the book. So that wasn't a good option. I certainly don't want to ask Cousin James. Maybe Cousin Abraham would give me some money. I could tell him that I need to buy school supplies. Then he'd ask Mama about it. So those weren't good options either.*

I really want to be friends with Zach and the other boys instead of being with my brothers all the time. The best way to do that is to take a risk and accept their invitation. After all, Uncle Abel owns the tavern and Mama can't object too much since he's family. First, I need to make sure Mama doesn't have anything else for me to do after school, also find a way to get some money to take with me.

A bright idea flashed through his mind. *The Christmas canister on the mantle! Cousin James puts coins in it when he comes home from the mill and Mama sometimes does too. I'll maybe borrow some of those coins for tomorrow and replace them from my earnings— maybe even add a few.*

The canister won't miss a few coppers and dimes, he convinced himself when he crept downstairs in the middle of the night to get the coins out of the canister. As he was putting the container back on the mantle a flickering candle appeared at the top of the stairs and, he heard Mama say, "Who's there?"

"Me, Mama, I woke up hungry and thought there might be some brown bread left from supper."

"Come back to bed. Your hungry stomach can wait. It's only two more hours until you have to get up to milk the cow anyway."

With a mixture of fear of being discovered, guilt from telling a lie, and elation that he now had the coins, Thad dutifully returned to his bed. Fortunately, Joshua didn't wake up. If he did, Thad knew he'd discover the money.

"Some of the boys at school asked me to meet them at the tavern after school. May I, Mama?" He asked her at breakfast.

"What for?" Cousin James wanted to know.

"To rehearse for our Shakespeare play," Thad lied.

"No drinking, no card games, and no betting on bulls," Mama warned. "They'll only get you into trouble."

"Too cold for bull-baiting," Thad mumbled as he collected his jacket and cap and left the house as fast as he could manage.

When Mrs. Hicks rang the school bell at one o'clock, Thad was dressed and ready to leave. Joshua handed Thad his script. In his haste he had forgotten to take it with him.

"Forget something?" Joshua pursed his lips and squinted in a look of disgust.

Thad took the script Joshua held out.

"Didn't think I'd need it since I've memorized my lines, but I'll take it with me anyway." He walked as fast as his bad foot would allow getting out from under his older brother's gaze.

When he entered the tavern, Thad searched around to find Zach and his friends.

"Looking for your friends?" Uncle Abel said pointing to the back of the tavern. When Thad found them he noted Zach shaking dice.

"We're playing "chuck-a-luck"," Zach explained. "All you have to do is guess what numbers will be shown on the dice when I throw them. We each take a turn guessing. You put as many coins down as you want on your guess. Whoever guesses correctly wins all the coins on the table. If no one wins, the coins stay until the next round. Ready?"

Thad nodded and sat down. Each boy announced his guess before the dice were rolled out on the table. Since he had so few coins, Thad put only one copper down on the table. No one's guess was correct on the first throw.

"Now all the coins on the table go in the middle. We go around the table. Each person gets a chance to roll the dice."

No one guessed correctly on the next round and the next, until all Thad's coins were gone.

Uncle Abel tapped him on the shoulder. "Got a message from your mother. She wants you to stop at the store on your way home to pick up a jar of molasses."

Saved by molasses.

"Sorry, have to go to the store for my mother. See you in school. Count me in if you're playing tomorrow. I intend to win tomorrow."

When Thad arrived home, he found two unfamiliar horses hitched to the post outside. *Maybe another cobbling order? Hope so. Then I can make some money to put the coins back in the canister.* But when he walked in the door Mama's stern visage greeted him. She steered him into the parlor. There sitting on the settee were the two bounty hunters.

"We didn't find those two runaways yet, but we will. Meanwhile we're here to present you with this citation for interfering with justice and for suspected harboring slaves." One of them retrieved a paper out of his satchel.

Mama took the citation and said, "My son is under age and has done nothing wrong. I'll give this citation to my brother who is a Justice of the Peace. Now, gentlemen, I'm asking you to leave this house." She escorted them to the door.

Despite the citation, Thad was relieved that he hadn't gotten a scolding. For the rest of that week, he disappeared after school. Every night he took more coins from the Christmas canister on the mantle. He played other dice games and one game of poker with his new friends at the tavern. At least now they wouldn't bully him. But he didn't earn back any of the coins he'd been borrowing. He only won the pot once and not enough to replenish the coins he'd been taking from the canister. Every day he dug his hole of deceit a little deeper.

The evening arrived when all parents were invited to attend their production of *Hamlet*. During dinner, Cousin James announced, "Since Christmas will be here in two weeks, I think it's time to see how much money we've saved for Christmas presents."

Thad gulped down his cider and coughed.

"You all right, Thad?" Mama asked.

"Just nervous." His words came out like he'd swallowed them instead of his food. *They can't look in that canister now—not before the play— not before I've replaced the coins I've taken out.* But it was too late. Cousin James dumped out onto the table the few coins left in the canister.

"What!" he shouted. He looked over at Mama. "Sarah, did you take the money out of the canister to use for the household? If so you could have asked me."

"No. James. I put coins in. I didn't take them out."

Joshua stared daggers at Thad. Thad clenched and un-clenched his hands on his lap. His innards tied up in knots.

Mama turned to look at Thad, her mouth dropped open, then she shook her head as if to brush away cobwebs. Abner and Alanson put their spoons down, yet their mouths remained open and they shook their heads from side to side. Cousin James stood up and pounded the table with his fist so that their plates leapt up and crashed down.

"Thad. You STOLE our Christmas money. How could you do this to your family?

"I...I just b-borrowed them...was plan...n...ing to pay...back," Thad stuttered and stammered out the words.

"That's it. I've had enough of you. Not only will you put the money back, you'll do so before Christmas. No school until you do and you can't live under my roof any longer."

"But, James, he has the lead role in the school play tonight," Mama pleaded. "He needs to go to school. Besides, where will he live and how will he pay back the money he borrowed before Christmas?"

"You figure it out, Sarah. He's your son—or I should say his father's son. He'll come to no good like him. I don't care if he's playing Shakespeare himself, I certainly won't attend. And no school starting tomorrow until he replaces the money he took; and furthermore, he's not to live in my home until he makes his amends."

Now that Thad had been exposed, the tightness in his chest eased a bit. He hated himself for lying. Once he started lying about going to the tavern to rehearse the play, one lie piled up on another and before he realized what he had been doing, lying had become a way of life. Mama had certainly taught him that playing cards and gambling were wrong in the eyes of the Lord. But all the men at the tavern gambled. Thad really didn't see why it was wrong especially since he liked the thrill of seeing if he could beat the odds. But his stealing money from the Christmas canister was wrong. *I'll put the coins I took back into the canister and, from now on, earn the money I gamble with. No school. That hurts. I'm the top student, after all. So I'll need to find a way to replace the money back fast. At least tonight, I'll be able to recite all the soliloquies I've memorized.*

Thad excused himself and climbed up the stairs to gather together his belongings to take with him. *I'll go live at our farm. Glad to get away from Cousin James' meanness.*

Mama followed him up the stairs.

"Thad, why did you steal coins from our Christmas canister? What did you use them for?"

I know why I did but I don't want to tell Mama as she won't approve of my gambling. I can invent another lie. No. Maybe she'll think that I bought a special Christmas present for her. He finally said, "I can't tell you."

"Well, I don't want you to miss too much school so I'm going to consult with Uncle Abel and Cousin Abraham to see how they can help you find a job and have a place to live."

"I plan to go live at the farm, Mama."

"No. I don't want you staying out there all alone and there's no way you could find a job out there this time of year. I'll go talk to Uncle Abel."

"See you after the play, then," Thad said, picking up his cane and a bundle of clothes and heading for the stairs. Mama took the bundle away from him.

"I'll bring this to you at the show tonight. Go on. I'll see you there."

Now she'll find out what I was doing at the tavern since Uncle Abel knows. My pit is deep and there's no easy way out.

"O, that this too solid flesh would melt, thaw, and resolve itself into a dew!"

I need my wit to find my way out, like Hamlet, Thad thought as he mounted Dawn and rode into town. *Maybe today I'll get lucky and meet Lucy and Festus.* Every day as he rode home from school or from the tavern he had been looking for his friend. Looking up from his reveries and still feeling sorry for himself, he noted in the distance two familiar figures climbing down from a wagon. Could it be them? Thad let Dawn have her lead and they cantered into town. "Thad," Lucy exclaimed, "How are you?"

"Not so good," he replied. "But as long as you're in town can you and Festus come to see me perform Hamlet tonight at my school?"

"My Pappy and Mammy are inside the store. Can they come too?"

"Don't see why not. Can we go somewhere and talk? How about the

Congregational Church over there. That's where we'll perform."

"Okay. I'll tell my parents and meet you there."

His heart bounced with joy. *Maybe Lucy can help me figure out my options.*

Mrs. Hicks was at the church with some of the other boys working on the scenery. "Hello Thad," she called. "Here to practice your lines?"

Thad nodded. "Mind if we sit back here in this last pew, my friend and I?"

She looked at Thad suspiciously and then turned back to supervising the scenery placement. Thad picked up his script and sat in the back pew with Lucy. He put his arm around her shoulders. She squirmed and turned her head away from him. Thad withdrew his arm and took a deep breath.

"Did the slave hunters come to your farm?"

"Yes. Pappy let them look around, showed him our freedom papers, and asked them to leave. They called him an uppity nigger and one of these days they'd come back to put him in his place, then left. I hid in the woods so they wouldn't see me or molest me."

"I got a citation for obstructing justice. Cousin Abraham has it now. Mama was mad. I'm nothing but trouble," Thad sighed and looked down at his feet. "Cousin James has kicked me out of his house."

"He kicked me out, too, remember?"

"Yes, but he had reason to kick me out. I stole the coins from our Christmas savings canister and I lied to them about going to the tavern to practice for the play tonight. I really went to gamble with some boys in my school and I lost all the money I stole. Now I have no place to live and have to get a job to replace the money I took. Mama will probably talk to my Uncle Abel and will find out I lied about why I was at the tavern."

"Maybe you can come and live at our farm. But we have no paying jobs for hire during the winter months."

They sat silently side my side for what seems like an eternity. Thad could hear the scraping of furniture and sets being moved.

"I can sell my horse, Dawn. Mama planned to sell her anyway."

"Then how would you get around?"

"Walk, I guess. If I can borrow snowshoes it won't be so bad."

Now I've chosen the best option to redeem myself, I feel like a burden has been lifted off my shoulders. I don't really want to think about losing my best 4-hooved friend – not now anyway. But I have to.

Thad decided to put up a sign at the post office the next day. Meanwhile, he would practice his soliloquies with Lucy.

CHAPTER NINETEEN

Moving Forward

"The play's the thing wherein I'll catch the conscience of the King."
Thad was at home in the role of Prince Hamlet, a man of many words, of intrigue and mystery. He had no trouble remembering his lines. Even his club foot didn't bother him—except it made performing as Hamlet more challenging. Playing the role of Hamlet, who was angry at Claudius, was so much like Thad being angry at Cousin James, *who thinks he's king.*

After the play parents and siblings in the audience applauded and the players took their bows. Thad overheard Mama talking to Uncle Abel. She threw up her hands in the air, her head back, and shouted, "What am I going to do with him!"

Uncle Abel shook his head, "Shouldn't have told you, Sarah. " When Thad joined them he only said, "Great performance as Hamlet, Thad."

Mama sent daggers Thad's direction and with her finger pointing right into his nose said, "You gambled…and…you lied!" She turned and walked away.

Cousin Abraham, who was standing nearby and had obviously overheard their conversation, said, "You're coming to live with me, Thad." He handed Thad his bag of belongings.

Uncle Abel put his hand on Thad's shoulder, "You can work for me until you pay back the money."

"Thanks for the offer, but it would be too much of a temptation to go back to the tavern right now," Thad replied. "I've decided to sell Dawn since Pappy gave her to me. That way I can replace the money and go back to school sooner."

Thad turned his head and looked over at Cousin Abraham, "But I would like to live with you, Cousin Abraham, and not go back to live with Cousin James."

Then Thad noted the sad expression in Uncle Abel's eyes. The pain was there. *I guess he doesn't get along with his own son sometimes.*

The very next day Thad put up a notice at the post office and gave one to Joshua to post at the cobbler shop. In only two days, Mr. Ashley, who had brought his two sons for Joshua and Thad to make their winter boots, came into the shop and told Joshua that he wanted to purchase Dawn. Joshua said he'd find Thad to tell him.

So at the agreed upon time, Mr. Ashley brought his oldest son to meet Thad at his Cousin Abraham's home and offered ten silver dollar coins to purchase Dawn.

When Mr. Ashley handed Thad the coins, Thad realized that he had enough to replenish what he had stolen from the Christmas canister with some left over.

He walked with the boy and his father outside to where Dawn was tethered. Then he handed the reigns over to Mr. Ashley, who took them and gave them to his son and said, "Here's your Christmas present, son."

"I'm going to miss you Dawn," Thad said rubbing her nose, his tears falling down and landing on her snout. He thought her eyes clouded over. She nuzzled him and whinnied softly.

"You'll have a good family to take care of you," he whispered in her ear. Then, not wanting the Ashleys to see his tears, he turned, brushed his hand over his face and said to the beaming boy, "Take good care of her. My pappy gave her to me when I was about your age."

Cousin Abraham motioned for Thad to climb into his wagon. Thad did so, his cheeks still wet. They drove in silence to Cousin James'. Mama opened the door.

"Oh, it's you," she said with ice in her voice. "Did you forget some-thing?"

Thad hesitated, looked down at his feet and said, *"I'm sorry, Mama."*

Then he said "Here's the amount I stole from the container. I sold Dawn to get the money. The rest is a little something extra for what you need for Christmas."

Thad looked up at her arms folded across her chest and wished they would hug him. Instead he held out his hands with the coins. She unfolded her arms and took them and put them in the pocket of her apron.

Thad then turned to leave.

"You're forgiven, son. Don't ever steal again. Return to your classes. I'll see if Cousin James will take you back."

"No, Mama," Thad replied. "I think I'll stay with Cousin Abraham for a while longer."

"At least come and spend Christmas with us," Mama said, "Abraham too."

So Thad agreed. He went with Cousin Abraham and his family to their home for Christmas Day. Susan and Catherine threw their arms around his waist. Cousin James shook his hand. Thad grasped Joshua's hands and gave Abram and Alanson each a hug.

When he opened his gifts, Thad found a set of snow shoes from Mama and some new pantaloons. The pantaloons he could do without but he now needed the snow shoes and hoped he could manage them with one club foot and his cane. Now every day the world around them was white and glistening. Icicles dripped from barn roofs and snow covered bushes and roads. Horses, Boston Boobys, cutters, and pods or sleds with runners carried folks around.

Although Thad wanted to visit Lucy and Festus, they lived too far away to get there with snow shoes.

"About Lucy Prince," Cousin Abraham said to Thad on Christmas night while they were sitting in front of the hearth in his parlor. The flicking flames crackled and Thad felt at peace after spending the day with the rest of his family.

"What about her?"

"Do you still see her?"

"I'd like to when I can."

"She's welcome to come here, even though she's not welcome at

Cousin James'. You don't have to meet in secret. In spite of the fact that many states still have laws forbidding blacks and whites to fraternize with each other, that's not true in Vermont.

"But Cousin James…"

"Even though some of our Vermont citizens still frown on blacks and whites being friends, I admire you for your commitment to equal rights, so ask her to come for dinner with her family."

Thad didn't ask Cousin Abraham to invite Jim and Claude. He hoped that after leaving Mr. Johnson's safe house in Peacham the two had made it to Canada before the snows blocked off all travel. Thad was pleased to know that many Vermonters didn't believe in slavery. Even though no one in town talked about it, many others did exactly what his family had done— helped runaway slaves secretly; all except Cousin James. He was such a big shot in town because of his owning so many businesses. Thad didn't know how Mama put up with him, housekeeping for him, and taking care of his girls. At least Thad didn't have to live with him, for now. Cousin Abraham was the only one, besides Pappy, who really understood and encouraged him. He didn't wrestle, like Pappy, but he bantered with him and Thad was less shy and less angry when he was around him.

Lucy, Festus, another brother and their parents and grandmother came for dinner on New Year's Day. Lucy's grandmother shared the story of how she argued before the Vermont Supreme Court to get back her husband's farm land that had been taken away from them. Cousin Abraham asked her all kinds of legal questions. Thad listened and absorbed her strategies. She wasn't even a lawyer and she had won her case in the Vermont Supreme Court! *Someday maybe I can argue and win a case before the Supreme Court.*

After vacation Thad rejoined the other boys at school. Cousin Abraham permitted him to work in his office after one o'clock. As Justice he dealt with men disturbing the peace when they got drunk. Cousin Abraham issued a fine and told each one to stay away from the tavern for a week. But they returned the very next week for the same offense. Each man reminded Thad of his pappy and how many times he'd come before a Justice of the Peace. *Maybe he's in jail somewhere now for not being able to pay the fines.* That happened to many men in Danville.

Sometimes a couple would come and ask to get married and Thad seized the opportunity to become one of their witnesses.

Cousin Abraham took Thad's citation from the slave hunters to the local sheriff. Thad told him that he had knocked the papers out of the slave hunter's hand because he was harassing Lucy. Cousin Abraham and the sheriff tore up the citation.

"Just let them try that again to any woman in this town," the sheriff fumed.

"They'll get more than a fine from me," Cousin Abraham added.

By March the sap ran from the maple trees and Mama invited Thad to join the family at their farm to tap the mature trees, put wooden buckets under the taps, and collect sap for syrup.

Rivulets of water coursed through the snow coming down from Lookout Mountain, winding their way to the nearby brooks during the day. At night the rivulets froze, only to thaw and start the process again the next day. As the trees thawed out from their winter freeze, they too sent out rivulets of watery sap that coursed through the tree trunks. The Indians who lived here before them had taught the Morrills how to tap the trees and make maple syrup.

"Abner, Alanson, Susan, and Catherine can collect the buckets. Thad, you take the barrels in the wagon to the sugaring building down the road," Mama told them.

The week at their farm sugaring went by much too quickly for Thad.

Mama took Joshua and Thad aside the last day as they were packing up the wagon and getting ready to return to town.

"Next week, we're going to take a ride over to Peacham to visit the Caledonia County Academy. Mrs. Hicks tells me that she has a hard time challenging you at the temporary grammar school.

"But Mama," Joshua said, "How can we afford to go to a school where we have to pay tuition?"

"And where will we live?" Thad asked.

"Well," Mama hesitated, "I have an offer from someone to purchase this farm, so we can pay off your father's debts and have some left over for tuition."

"No!" Thad screamed," I love our farm!"

"Thad," I know how much the farm means to you— to all of us. But your education is more important than the farm."

"And what about our cobbler shop?" Joshua added.

"We'll see about that. First, we need to find out if they will accept you both as students for the coming school year."

"Can I ride out one more time through the pasture to say goodbye to Lookout Mountain?"

"Yes. Take Gerty," Mama said as she continued to pile up their belongings into the wagon.

Thad mounted Gerty and nudged her forward with his good heel. They passed maple trees that gave up their sap, evergreens shaking off winter snows, and stone walls meandering their way on either side of the meadow. His mind, too, meandered, lingering over lessons learned during the past year. He said goodbye to Lookout Mountain, then trotted back to say goodbye to the familiar farmhouse and weather-beaten barn. Now that the calendar had turned to 1806, he knew he had learned much about himself. With the promise of attending a real school in a new town, he turned his back to the farm, filled with anticipation of what would lie ahead.

CHAPTER TWENTY

Lydia Smith's Reflections

Sixty-three years have gone by since the story about his thirteenth year in Vermont circulated. Mr. Stevens is now lying in his bed here in a house in Washington where he's been since that last tumultuous session of Congress. He says he's glad someone wrote down all that happened so long ago because he has been preoccupied since then.

I've been his housekeeper for twenty years now and have been taking care of him since he's been so ill. He tells me story after story about Lookout Mountain, their farm near there, and how he hated selling Dawn.

"No horse after Dawn meant as much to me as that filly did."

When Mr. Stevens earned enough money from his law practice and his various business enterprises, he bought a dairy farm in Peacham for his Mama and visited her there often. His Mama raised Thad and his brothers after his father left. She made sure that her four boys received the best schooling and she instilled in all of them the importance of education. His older brother Joshua was a cobbler and a justice and Abner, a physician. Mr. Stevens took up his Mama's cause of the importance of a good education and has become a staunch advocate of education for everyone.

Mr. Stevens and his brothers attended the Caledonia Academy in Peacham when it opened. In fact, his Cousin James purchased a home in

Peacham after he remarried. Thad's mama kept house in James' Peacham house so her boys could attend the school. However, Thad did get into trouble there just as he had when he attended school in Danville. After he graduated from the Academy he attended Dartmouth College. He spent a year at the University of Vermont, returning to Dartmouth for his college graduation.

Mr. Stevens has this tendency to take risks and his smart mouth and sharp tongue often turn people against him. On the other hand, his keen mind and wit have gotten him far in life, even though his enemies think differently. While he was attending Dartmouth he managed to get himself out of a scrape with a cow through his quick thinking and legal posturing. Many admire him for speaking his mind on matters important to him, and that's why he's been reelected to Congress so many times. But his enemies didn't like it when he called them "skunks with foul putrid odor."

So many of Mr. Stevens' immediate family have died. He lost his brother Abner and his sister-in-law, Lucy Stevens, first. Abner and Thaddeus were very close, so when both Abner and his wife died, Mr. Stevens took in their two boys, Thaddeus Jr. and Alanson and raised them along with my children. Those two boys are like sons to him, since he didn't have any children of his own because he never married. His nephew Alanson died in the War Between the States. Joshua, too, is dead.

Thaddeus, Jr. is now by his uncle's bedside while I finish writing. He has joined his uncle in the practice of law.

Mr. Stevens liked several other women, besides Lucy Prince, he told me. He even had several housekeepers before me. He says that I'm the only housekeeper who lasted because I can put up with his sarcastic wit and bad temper. We've developed a strong business relationship over the many years I've been working for him. I now have my own house next to his and a business, too. He says I remind him of his late mother, because I keep his life orderly, like she did.

He never really found out what happened to his father. Talk was that he died in the War of 1812. For many years Mr. Stevens refused to discuss much about his father, especially during the first ten years that I worked for him. He recently admitted that he had mixed up feelings toward him, much like slaves have for their masters. He was angry at his pappy for a long time for leaving his family in debt. Nevertheless, his father had been his best friend so he missed him. The little he has shared with me about his father, I think Mr. Stevens is very much like him. He certainly inherited his tendencies to drink and gamble. After I came to work for him, one day he threw away all his bottles of liquor and wrote Thaddeus, Jr. to do the same. This nephew first got in trouble with the intoxicating drink when he was at Dartmouth College. He still can't stay sober and Mr. Stevens is very concerned about him. I've read that Dr. Benjamin Rush believes that some men have an allergy to alcohol. I guess that could be true about the Stevens boys. Mr. Stevens still likes to gamble. After stealing the money from the Christmas canister, he now doesn't gamble unless he earns the money to cover his bets. Still, I've warned him that one day he might not be able to pay his gambling debts and then what?

Though he didn't get along with his Cousin James, his Cousin Abraham became his first substitute father and mentor. He had other mentors as well, John Mattocks tutored him in Law in Peacham; David Cassalt, while he taught school in York, Pennsylvania. Following their example he was able to become a surrogate father for his two nephews.

He tells me how very religious his mother was, making sure he knew the Bible and the Creeds, but the church going didn't stick. He says he'd rather go to a tavern than sit on a hard pew on Sundays. He says he doesn't need that kind of religion because his Mama taught him more about Christian love and caring for others by her example. She also instilled in all of her sons that we're all equal in the sight of the Lord. Knowing that he is now so sick, however, I had Mr. Stevens baptized in the Catholic faith to be sure he is prepared for his death. This is how he wants to be remembered when he dies:

"Here lies one who never rose to any eminence, and who only courted the low ambition to have it said that he had striven to ameliorate the condition of the poor, the lowly, the downtrodden of every race and language and color."[7]

Glossary of Words, Terms and Idioms

Be that as it may *is another way of saying even though that is true the problem needs to be solved.*

Boston Booby *was an enclosed coach on runners or sleds for winter use. Other sleighs were* **Pods,** *a one horse sleigh, and* **Cutters,** *made to hold more than one person.*

Bull-baiting *was a barbaric form of entertainment in which dogs were let loose on a tethered bull behind a tavern. It involved gambling.*

Burnished *was a process whereby rough cow or deer hide can be made smooth and shining with a glazing tool like a screw driver by a* **cobbler** *or shoe-maker. Other cobblers tools were:* **pinchers** *like pliers; a* **last, a** *wood or metal mold; an* **awl,** *to punch holes so a needle with thread made from waxed plant fibers could sew the pieces together.*

Chip of the old block *came to be chip off the old block meaning the child resembles his parent.*

Chuck-a-luck *was a gambling game involving betting on numbers on three thrown dice.*

Coloured person *was a name given to a slave or former slave, also called* **Negro.** *Derogatory names were nigger or* **nigger-lover.** *A* **Mulatto** *was the offspring of a black person and a white person.*

Conestoga wagon *was a large covered wagon that carried persons and belongings.*

Dang *and* **Tarnation** *are swear words for damn*

Esq. (Esquire) *at the end of one's name signifies that the person passed a bar examination to become a lawyer.*

Golden key can open any door *is an English Elizabethan phrase that means that money can buy anything.*

Huzzah *is the same as Hurrah.*

In a pickle *is an English phrase for being in a difficult situation.*

Little end of the horn *means to come out of a situation disadvantaged.*

Parchment *is a kind of paper made from the skin of a goat or sheep.*

Paying the piper *means to pay the consequences for one's actions.*

Put on a thinking cap *means to concentrate on thinking.*

Put hair on your chest *means thinking that strong drink can help you grow into being a man.*

Pay any mind *means not paying any attention.*

Settee *is a medium sized sofa with arms and a back.*

Streaked *is another term for frightened or annoyed.*

Tons of rocks *means having lots of money, usually coins for betting.*

Vittles or victuals *is another word for food.*

Whitewash *means to hide one's faults or shortcomings.*

Appendices

The Legislative Process in Vermont

In 1805 when the Vermont Assembly met in Danville to pass legislation pertaining to their fourteenth state, Vermont had a single legislative body of delegates from each region of the state. The executive branch, comprised of the Governor and the Council, also met at the same time, although in a different place. Two hundred delegates brought petitions with them prepared in their town or region. They also raised their own monies for room and board and stayed in the local inn and the homes of twenty residents of the town. Their petitions were deliberated in committees during a month long session and approved by the Governor and the Council. The Governor and the Council also sent their suggestions to the legislators for their consideration. Because of the importance of dairy farming to Vermont, each delegation had to include a dairy farmer. During the 1805 Assembly delegates chose Montpelier as their state capital, although the building for housing the legislature was not completed until 1808.

Vermont Senator Bradley introduced the slave trade cessation legislation to the American Congress. His bill, the federal "Act to Prohibit the Importation of Slaves," was enacted also in 1808 and was signed into law by President Thomas Jefferson.

Today the Vermont Legislature meets in Montpelier and consists of two houses, the Senate and the House of Representatives. There are 180 members in all; 30 Senators and 150 Representatives, based on population. Senators and Representatives are paid a weekly salary when the House and Senate are in session. Committees can have at least two readings of proposed bills before a vote.

Henry Little began the tradition of having legislative pages, a job open to boys thirteen and fourteen. No historical record exists that Thaddeus Stevens was actually a page during the 1805 legislative session in Danville.

The Importance of Education

In this story, Thaddeus' mother, Sarah Stevens, expresses the importance of education when she repeats the phrase that education will be "the key to unlock any door." Mrs. Stevens, an impoverished single mother, had to work as a housekeeper and nurse to get enough money to be able to pay the school fees for Joshua and Thaddeus to attend the Peacham Academy School created by the Vermont General Assembly in 1805. During that time period parents needed to pay fees for their children to attend any school.

The free public education movement did not begin until the 1830s, during the time that Thaddeus Stevens was a Pennsylvania legislator. Up until that time there were practically no free public schools. When a Free School Bill was introduced in the Pennsylvania House of Representatives, lawyer Stevens became an ardent supporter. However, it took two tries in the legislative process to pass the Free School Act in the Pennsylvania General Assembly. Thanks to Thaddeus Stevens' determination, Pennsylvania made education available to everyone before New York, New Jersey, Connecticut, Rhode Island, and even the entire Southern states.

Attorney Stevens wanted education to be available to anyone, anywhere no matter what his/her circumstances of life might be. When he was a student at Dartmouth College, Thaddeus never had enough money to purchase textbooks and was made an outcast by the richer students. Even though he was more qualified than most of his peers, he was not nominated for Phi Beta Kappa, an honors fraternity.

As a teacher himself—first at Peacham and then in York, Pennsylvania—Mr. Stevens was a strong advocate for every child's education. When he became wealthy as a lawyer in Pennsylvania, he helped many poor students acquire an education. He believed that education was the great equalizer. He later said that if you make education inexpensive and honorable, a person with intelligence, no matter how poor, would utilize that opportunity to improve himself.

In his will Thaddeus Stevens left $50,000 to establish a school for the relief and refuge of homeless, indigent orphans. He directed that:

"They shall be carefully educated in the various branches of English education and all industrial trades and pursuits. No preference shall be shown on account of race or color in their admission or treatment. Neither poor Germans, Irish or Mahometan, nor any others on account of their race or religion of their parents, shall be excluded. They shall be fed at the same table."[8]

Many elementary and middle schools in Pennsylvania, New York, Vermont, and Washington, DC are also named for "The Great Commoner," as he became known. In Vermont, Thaddeus Stevens School in Lyndon Center, Vermont (formerly The Stevens School in Peacham) came into existence as a middle school by the authority of the State Legislature in 1999. The school's admiration for what Thaddeus Stevens stood for informs their deep commitment to civil and human rights. Scholarships provide an open door for families who cannot afford to pay the whole tuition.

The Thaddeus Stevens College of Technology in Lancaster, Pennsylvania first started as a school as specified in Thaddeus Stevens' will. In 1905 an act of the Pennsylvania Legislature publicly funded the school and in 1998 it became a college. At that time the college began granting a two-year associate of applied science degree in fifteen programs. Eighty-six percent of the students who are accepted receive financial aid through state and federal government grants and loans. In addition, some students receive additional funds, thanks to the tireless fund raising efforts of the Thaddeus Stevens Foundation. Today, twenty-one programs provide opportunities for economically disadvantaged and academically qualified students to acquire an education in technology and the trades.

Disabilities and Diseases: Yesterday and Today

In this story, both Thaddeus and his brother, Joshua, were born with club feet—a medical condition called Congenital Talipes Equinovarus—considered a disability today. In 1805 no one knew the cause of why babies were born with this abnormality and no treatment was available to make the foot more normal. Consequently, children who were born with this condition or any other, including a wide spectrum of brain disorders, were considered outcasts and fell prey to bullying and their parents to being ostracized.

Today treatment for club feet is started when the disabled child is an infant. A procedure called the Ponseti method of stretching and casting may alleviate the condition. However, often the pain persists and the affected person cannot be on his feet for any long period of time. The First Step is an international not for profit organization that raises funds for treating children with this condition in developing countries.

In 1805 no treatment existed for those born with other medical conditions causing behavioral and societal problems, such as the inherited and environmental brain diseases of addiction to alcohol and gambling. Boys were encouraged to drink alcoholic beverages as a rite to manhood, but if you got drunk you were a sinner. Drunkenness became such a problem that the Washingtonian Temperance Societies, with pledges for abstinence, came into existence.

Today, with advances in neurological research, proof exists that due to inherited brain abnormalities, men especially, are susceptible to becoming addicted; women, on the other hand, have an insufficient amount of an enzyme called Alcohol Dehydrogenase to be able adequately to process alcohol into its constituent components. Instead, women's brains are impacted by the alcohol sooner than men's. Spiritual recovery support groups, such as Alcoholics Anonymous and Gamblers Anonymous, and special rehabilitation centers provide treatment options that work for affected individuals. All family members, such as the Stevens family, suffer from the behaviors of the addict. They need counseling treatment and support groups as well. The evidence of the effectiveness of such treatment did not become known until the 1970s.

The Americans with Disabilities Act (ADA) of 1990 prohibits discrimination against people with disabilities in employment, transportation, public accommodation, communications, and governmental activities. Public schools are now required to challenge students with disabilities to excel in the general curriculum and bullying of such students, punishable. Instructional aides and supports for learning have become standard in most schools.

Essay by Thao Nguyen, 2013 Winner of Fifth Grade Thaddeus Stevens Foundation Essay Contest

"Change is the end result of all true learning," is a quote by Leo Buscaglia. Thaddeus Stevens changed the way education was delivered to people because of his true learning opportunities. His pursuit for knowledge led him to gain not only education but wisdom. Thaddeus Stevens wanted to provide public education to those who couldn't have access. He wanted to give them the same opportunity as he was given at a young age.

Thaddeus Stevens didn't have luxuries of life in the beginning. His father was an alcoholic and an abusive man who left the family when Thaddeus was only twelve-years-old. His family was poor, but his mother worked hard. Despite their poor condition she was able to provide education to Thaddeus and his siblings by scraping up all the money she had. Because of Thaddeus Stevens' mother, he was able to lead a successful life. Her sacrifice and compassion toward him allowed Thaddeus Stevens to do the same for others who were unprivileged as he was at a young age. While attending school Thaddeus Stevens was bullied. He had poor physical qualities, but he excelled in school. He went to Dartmouth College and was the smartest student. Being an outcast didn't stop him from achieving success in life. He studied law and passed the bar exam in a year. He practiced in Gettysburg and later moved to Lancaster where he would become an instant success. Thaddeus was able to argue nine out of ten cases before the Pennsylvania Supreme Court and after five years he owned a house, properties, and purchased a farm for his mother with fourteen cows. In the next twenty-one years he became very wealthy as an excellent attorney, politician, and philanthropist. Overall his success displays that bullying can never get in the way. It's simply an obstacle that can be overcome with time, because knowledge is powerful and success tastes sweeter with it. Thaddeus realized that many people are being outcast from society. He disliked exclusionary clubs because some excluded cripples. He saw that only families that can afford to send children to school did so. It's only when a poor child's family would admit poverty in public would they be able to attend. Education is something with no boundaries, yet Thaddeus Stevens saw education being held as a luxury where it should be held as a necessity. Education discriminated and segregated the people based on how much money they had as well as race. Mr. Stevens supported the Free School Bill which was later passed. Public education spread to New York, New Jersey, Connecticut, Rhode Island, and the entire South. What started out with true learning ended with a change. Thaddeus Stevens had a tough beginning, had been bullied, but despite all the shortcomings, he was able to change education. He opened up many doors of opportunities for people who were like him, regardless of a person's age, race, and gender. Learning is an equal right because with the right knowledge can lead to right changes. It doesn't matter where one comes from, but how they take advantage of opportunities given in life. Thaddeus Stevens' life started as a spark and he was able to ignite the same spark in other lives."

Bibliography

Primary Sources

Gilbertson, Elsa. *Vermont Division for Historic Preservation.* www. Retrieved from http://www.livingplaces.com/Vt.html.

Journal for the General Assembly of State of Vermont 1805. Retrieved from http://catalog.hathitrust.org/Record/008606467.

Records of the Governor and Council of the State of Vermont.

October, 1805 to October, 1806. Vol. 5. retrieved from http://catalog.hathitrust.org/Record/007704675.56-99.

Records of the Governor and Council of the State of Vermont, Vol. 3, Appendix H. Retrieved from http://www.archive.org/details/records of governor verm.421ff.

Secondary Sources

Brabson, Kathy. *Life of Thad Stevens,* Yurchak Printing, Landisville, PA. 2013.

Brodie, Faun. *Thaddeus Stevens.* Vail-Ballau Press. 1959.

19th Century Education. *The History of Education in America.* Retrieved from http://www.chesapeake.edu/library/edu_101/eduhist_19thC. asp.

Chouinard, Paul. *Thaddeus Stevens in the Limelight.* A twenty-six page article written online by a member of the Danville Historical Society and sent by author.

Cohen, Lester. *Foreword to David Ramsey's the History of the American Revolution, vol. 1 in 1789.* Downloaded from http://www.use.jhu/books/9781614878568, also http://www.muse.jhu/books/9781614878568.

Cohen, Lester, Ed. *History of the American Revolution. vol.2. The state of the parties; the advantages and disadvantages of the Revolution; its influence on the minds and morals of the citizens.* Appendix IV. Retrieved from http://www.oll.libertyfund.org.

Education, US. *Encyclopedia of Children and Childhood History and Society.* Retrieved from http://www.faqs.org/childhood/Co-Fa/Education-United-States.html.

Epidemics: *The Deadly Cases that have plagued us for centuries. Rocky Mountain Spotted Fever: Description.* Retrieved from:http://www.Library.thinkquest.org/07/aug/00867/kate/1800s.html.

General Thaddeus Kosciusko. *Famous People.* Retrieved from http://polskiinternet.com/english/info/thadeuskosciuszko.html.

Gerina, Gretchen Holbrook. *Mr. and Mrs. Prince.* Harper Collins ebooks.

Hoch, Bradley R. *Thaddeus Stevens in Gettysburg. The Making of an Abolitionist.* Adams County Historical society.

Lancaster Historical Society. *Thaddeus Stevens and Slavery.* Vol. 15. #6.

McCutcheon, Marc. *Everyday Life in the 1800s.* Writers Digest Books. 1993.

Meltzer, Milton. *Thaddeus Stevens and the fight for Negro Rights.* Thomas Crowell Co., New York. 1967.

Shoe Shop, *Old Sturbridge Village. Shoemaking.* Retrieved from http://ab.mec.edu/departments/techinteg/resources/students/newlife/shoemaking.htm.

Susan, Bettye, et.al. "19th Century 1800-1809". *American Cultural History.* Lone Star College-Kingwood Library. Retrieved from http://www.appskc.lonestart.edu/popculture/19thcentury1800.htm.

Sustereeren, Dick Van. *In this state: Stevens, a Vermont Abolitionist Hero, Makes a Comeback on the Big Screen.* in <u>Life in Vermont</u>. January 13, 2013. http://Vtdigger.org.

Ramsey, David. "Advantages of the Revolution."

Trefousee, Hans L. *Thaddeus Stevens. Nineteenteeth Century Egalitarian.* University of North Carolina Press. 1997.

Woodburn, James Albert. *The Life of Thaddeus Stevens: A Study of American Political History.* Bobbs-Merrill Co. 1913.

Endnotes

1. Quote from Woodburn, *The Life of Thaddeus Stevens: A Study of American Political History.* 53 & 54.

2. Ramsey, *"Advantages of the Revolution."* 631.

3. *Ibid.* Foreword.

4. Vermont Legislative Journal record from 1805. 15.

5. *Ibid.* 35.

6. Mark 10:4-6 KJV.

7. *Thaddeus Stevens' journal.* Jan 13, 1865. 139 & 140.

8. From Thaddeus Stevens' will on file in Thaddeus Stevens College Archives.

CPSIA information can be obtained at www.ICGtesting.com
Printed in the USA
BVOW05s1334260315

393324BV00003B/4/P

9 781941 746110